CENTERVILLE

orca sports

CENTERVILLE

JEFF RUD

ORCA BOOK PUBLISHERS

Library and Archives Canada Cataloguing in Publication

Rud, Jeff, 1960–, author
Centerville / Jeff Rud.
(Orca sports)

Issued in print and electronic formats.
ISBN 978-1-4598-1031-0 (paperback).—ISBN 978-1-4598-1032-7 (pdf).—
ISBN 978-1-4598-1033-4 (epub)

I. Title. II. Series: Orca sports
PS8635.U32C45 2016   jC813'.6   C2015-904520-7
C2015-904521-5

First published in the United States, 2016
Library of Congress Control Number: 2015946333

Summary: In this high-interest sports novel, Jake Burnett must choose between
advancing his basketball career and doing the right thing when he uncovers the
truth about prestigious Centerville Prep.

*Orca Book Publishers is dedicated to preserving the environment and has printed
this book on Forest Stewardship Council® certified paper.*

Orca Book Publishers gratefully acknowledges the support for its publishing
programs provided by the following agencies: the Government of Canada
through the Canada Book Fund and the Canada Council for the Arts,
and the Province of British Columbia through the BC Arts Council
and the Book Publishing Tax Credit.

Cover photography by iStock.com
Author photo by Deborah McCarron

ORCA BOOK PUBLISHERS
www.orcabook.com

Printed and bound in Canada.

19 18 17 16 • 4 3 2 1

For Lana, Maggie and Matt—
the real home team.

Chapter One

"Ladies and gentlemen, this is the captain speaking. On behalf of the crew, I want to welcome you aboard flight 593 and let you know that we've got clear skies this afternoon. We'll be flying at an altitude of forty thousand feet. Given current wind conditions, we're expecting to land in Union City right on schedule, at about five thirty local time. So sit back and enjoy the flight..."

I barely heard what the captain was saying. I was too excited. This was it. I was finally on my way.

The past month had been a whirlwind with all the little things I needed to do to get ready for this trip. But in other ways, time had sometimes seemed liked it was dragging by. I was so jacked about going to Centerville Prep. I couldn't wait to get there.

I looked down at the rumpled brochure in my hand. On the cover was a picture of a white kid in midair, tossing a no-look pass. In my mind, that kid was me. I pictured a hulking teammate gobbling up my pass and jamming it home. I was itching to get on the court at Centerville. This was going to be sick!

It was hard to believe that I was actually on a plane, by myself, heading off to live hundreds of miles away from my home, my parents and my dog. Every few seconds I felt a tiny wave rippling across the bottom of my stomach. Somewhere deep inside, I admitted to myself that this was all kind of scary too. But that feeling was way deep down, where nobody else could see it. Mostly I was just excited.

The Centerville Prep Cougars were one of the top basketball teams in the entire country. And I was actually going there, to play my final year of high-school basketball. It seemed almost too good to be true. I glanced down again at the blue-and-red Centerville brochure. By now I had its contents memorized. *Growing elite basketball players and people,* it said in italicized white letters across the blue background of the cover.

Inside the brochure were pictures of the school's modern-looking dorms, cafeteria buffet tables loaded with food and drinks, and a chart with the previous season's national prep rankings listing Centerville at number 6. The chart included every one of the scores from the previous year's 28–8 team record. The Cougars had crisscrossed the country and even played against LeBron James's old high school.

In the center of the brochure, spanning the middle two pages, was a picture of the

Cougars' gleaming home basketball court. It looked much more like a college facility than a high-school gym, with at least ten rows of theater-style seating on either side. Across both baselines of the blond-hardwood court, the word *Cougars* was spelled out in royal blue on a bold red background. In the middle of the court stood two players proudly holding basketballs atop a gigantic logo—the growling head of a cougar. I imagined how good it would feel to dribble the ball across that shiny court, setting up the offense in front of hundreds of fans.

"Excuse me." The man sitting beside me nudged my right arm. "Can I get out to use the restroom?"

"Sure." I nodded, barely looking at him as I stood up to let him pass. I was too preoccupied with my adventure ahead to pay much attention.

It hadn't been easy talking Mom and Dad into letting me make this move. But once Coach Stone had shown up at my playoff game in the spring, asking if I was interested in attending his prep school for my senior year, I knew that somehow I had to get to Centerville.

My parents had needed a lot of convincing. They didn't see why I couldn't just finish out high school in Midland, playing for the Tigers again. After all, I had started as point guard for Midland and been all-district as a junior. *It's so far away from home,* was Mom's first reaction. *If you're good enough, the college scouts will find you,* was Dad's.

I had to agree with Mom. Centerville Prep was far away—nearly a thousand miles from the place I had lived my whole life up till now. But I totally disagreed with Dad. He just didn't understand basketball and how important it was for me to get noticed. Playing in the small town of Midland against single-A schools in the region, I had already become a dominant player. But who cared? Lots of friends and families came to our games, but I had never seen any college scouts in the gym.

In fact, the only scout I had ever seen at Midland was Coach Stone. He had been very optimistic about my chances of landing a college scholarship when he saw me play. He tracked me down outside the locker room afterward. *You need some exposure,* he told me. *You need to compete against real athletes every day. You need elite coaching. If you get all that, who knows how far you can go?*

Coach Stone's words from several months ago were still ringing in my ears when I was nudged again. "Excuse me," said the man, now returned from the restroom.

"No problem." I smiled, getting up again to let him back to his seat.

"You heading off to school somewhere— to college?" the man asked, glancing down at the brochure in my hands.

"Prep school," I replied. "I'm going to play at Centerville Prep for my senior high school season." The words still didn't seem quite real.

"Wow." The man smiled. "I can't say I've heard of that school. But you seem pretty excited about it. Good for you."

"Thanks. Yeah, I really am," I said, passing him the brochure and launching into a speech about Centerville Prep and its dorms, food, coaching and national schedule.

"Looks impressive," the man said, sliding his glasses down his nose and leafing carefully through the brochure. He was about Dad's age, maybe fifty, with salt-and-pepper hair. He wore a gray suit jacket with an open-collared black shirt.

"What about you?" I asked. "Where are you going?"

"Nowhere that exciting," he said. "I work for the State Board of Education. I'm heading back to Union City to get ready for another school year. Wanna trade places?"

I grinned. "Maybe not."

"Bill Jennings," the man said, extending his right hand to shake. "Nice to meet you."

"I'm Jake," I said. "Jake Burnett."

"Well, Jake," Bill said, "I'll remember that name. Maybe I'll hit you up for tickets when you make it to the NBA."

We both laughed. I hoped he was right. Although I had never actually told anybody, the NBA was my ultimate goal. It was just a long way off. Getting to Centerville was one giant step closer though.

"One piece of advice for you," Bill said. "Keep your focus on school too. Basketball is important. But school is just as important— probably more important in the long run."

"Thanks." I nodded. I knew it was good advice. It sounded like something my dad would say. But school wasn't what I was thinking about right now.

I slipped in my earbuds and found some old-school Jay Z on my phone—"Empire State of Mind." The song always reminded me of basketball and the big time. That's where I was headed. I just knew it.

Chapter Two

I scanned the luggage carousel underneath the numbers 593 in the crowded Union City International Airport. No bags on it yet. I hoped I wouldn't have to keep my driver waiting too long.

Coach Stone had said a driver would pick me up at the airport and take me the thirty miles to Benson, the suburban community where Centerville Prep was located. But I needed my bags first.

I had packed light. One large suitcase packed with clothes, shoes and other things I would need for school. My Nike Elite backpack was filled with basketball stuff, my laptop and school supplies. After a few bags appeared on the carousel, I saw a suitcase with a blue-tartan luggage tag topple onto the belt. My mom had insisted on attaching the family tartan luggage tag so I'd recognize it. That was my suitcase for sure.

A couple of minutes later, down came my bright-yellow backpack with the Midland Tigers crest on it. Soon, maybe by tomorrow even, I'd be getting all my Centerville gear. Then I could retire this backpack. I still liked it, but I was excited to trade it in for the red and blue of my new prep school.

I grabbed both bags and headed out to the airport pickup area. I was supposed to look for a driver holding up a sign that said *Jake Burnett*. I didn't see anybody with that sign. So I sat down on an empty bench and surveyed the area. Still nobody. No big deal. I could wait.

After several minutes of sitting, I heard my name being called over the airport PA system. "Paging passenger Jake Burnett. Jake Burnett, please pick up courtesy phone three."

This was weird. Who would be calling me at the airport? I had noticed the courtesy phones on my way to the baggage area, so I walked back toward them. I picked up a receiver and punched in line three.

"Hello?" I didn't know who to expect on the other end.

"Jake?" said a hurried voice. "Coach Stone here. Look, there's been a mix-up with the drivers today. We're going to have to get you to take the bus out here to Benson."

"Umm, okay," I said. "How do I do that?"

"Look for the ground transportation ticket window," Coach said. "It's not far from the luggage-pickup area. Then buy a ticket to Benson Station. I'll pick you up when you get here. It shouldn't take long."

Feeling a little relieved, I said, "Okay, thanks, Coach. See you soon." He had already hung up.

I found the bus-ticket window without any problem, but the lineup was at least ten people deep. I looked up at the board. It was a $22-one-way fare to Benson. Lucky thing Mom had insisted on giving me $200 spending money just in case.

By the time I got to the front of the line, the cashier had some more bad news. "Sorry," she said. "You just missed the bus to Benson. The next one goes in two hours."

Two hours? By now it was almost seven in the evening. I hadn't eaten since lunchtime, with Mom and Dad back in Midland. I collected my bus ticket and found a vending machine. I bought two granola bars and an apple juice with the change I had. This would have to do for now.

I had to admit that I was a little disappointed in the way things were going so far. No driver, having to take the bus, a long layover. It wasn't exactly how I had envisioned arriving at Centerville Prep. But I shook it off, slipped in my earbuds and took a seat. I rested my head against my yellow backpack. Before I knew it, the long silver Greyhound with *Benson* in the destination display was pulling up to the bus stop.

Thirty minutes later the bus wheeled into Benson Station. By now it was nearly ten o'clock and very dark outside. As I got off the bus and collected my bags from the sidewalk, I noticed Coach Stone standing a few feet away. He hadn't seen me yet.

"Hey, Coach!" I said, extending my hand to shake his. "Good to see you."

The coach, a burly man in his early fifties, wore a red-and-blue Centerville pullover. He shook my hand quickly. "Where have you been, Jake?" he said, a hint of annoyance in his voice. "I've been waiting here for two hours."

I was taken aback. "Sorry, Coach," I stammered. "I missed the bus because of the lineup at the airport, and this was the next one available."

He must have sensed my disappointment, because his square facial features softened and he smiled. "That's okay, son.

No problem. It's late though. We'll have to get you right to the house. School starts first thing tomorrow."

I nodded. I was happy to see that Coach wasn't going to stay mad at me. I mean, what could I have done any differently? He pointed me in the direction of a late-model blue minivan parked about a hundred feet away. On the side of the door it said *Centerville Prep* in red letters over the image of a basketball.

"Did you have a good flight, son?" Coach Stone said as he pulled out of the bus-station parking lot.

"Yes, it was fine," I said. "I was pretty excited to get here."

The coach didn't respond. We drove mostly in silence except for the sports-talk radio playing so low in the background that I couldn't tell what the announcers were saying. After just a five-minute drive in the dark, we pulled off into a residential neighborhood. Finally, we stopped in front of a small white house on a street full of similar-looking homes. A chain-link fence surrounded the yard. I could hear dogs barking loudly nearby.

"Okay, this is it," Coach Stone said. "We're here."

I looked out. Where exactly were we? This didn't look like the dorm in the brochure. And where was the school?

"Come on, Jake," Coach said. "Grab your bags, and I'll introduce you to some of the guys."

I followed the coach up the cracked concrete sidewalk. He opened the screen door, which was hanging awkwardly off one hinge. He knocked once on the main door before opening it and walking inside. I was a couple of steps behind.

The dimly lit living room contained two beat-up black leather sofas and one brown recliner, arranged in front of a good-sized projection TV screen. Four kids in baggy shorts and T-shirts were sprawled on the two sofas, one holding a game controller and playing *NBA 2K*, and the others watching the screen. A fifth boy sat in the recliner, feet outstretched, dangling lime-green Adidas flip-flops and holding the other game controller. He was wearing red Nike shorts and no shirt. He was taller than the rest, black and chiseled. Even though he was sitting down, I could sense this kid was very, very strong.

"What's good, gentlemen?" Coach Stone said as he arrived. The players sat up and all nodded hello. "Guys, this is your other roommate. This is Jake."

I felt so awkward. Here I was in the middle of a living room with five complete strangers. I felt every eye on me. I didn't know where to look. For a couple of seconds nobody said anything.

"Hey," said the big kid sitting in the recliner as he eyed me up and down. "What's up, man?"

I didn't have a chance to answer before Coach Stone interjected.

"Jake's a point guard from Midland," he said. "We're expecting big things from him."

The four boys on the sofas eyed me skeptically. I could tell that each of them was sizing me up.

"Shoot, Coach, you say that about every one of these kids you drop off," the big kid said, grinning. "We should be winning nationals if they're all as good as you say." The other boys laughed. I felt myself squirming.

"Thomas, I can always count on you having an opinion." Coach Stone smiled. "But we'll see, boys—maybe we *will* win nationals."

Coach looked at me and motioned with his eyes toward a room off the living room. "You'll be staying in there, with Thomas," he said. "Come on, bring your stuff. I'll show you."

I was relieved to leave the living room and escape the eyes of the boys on the sofas. We entered the bedroom. Against one wall was a single bed with a small chest of drawers set at one end. A pillow rested on top of the chest. "That's Thomas's bed," Coach said. "He needs the extension for his legs. Sleeping comfortably isn't easy when you're six foot eleven."

Six foot eleven and his name was Thomas? Wait a second, was I actually sharing a room with Thomas Delane? The number 2-ranked prep center in the entire country? I had read on the basketball chat boards that the kid was at Centerville, but I hadn't been sure until now. This was unreal!

"And this is your bed," Coach said, pointing to a cot on the other side of the room. "You can store your stuff in this closet. Thomas has some of his junk in there too."

I looked at the bed and surveyed the small bedroom. There was nothing hanging on the faded blue walls. The brown linoleum floor had definitely seen better days. One small window looked out onto the street where we had parked. It was a far cry from the dorms pictured in the Centerville brochure. It wasn't nearly as nice as my bedroom back home. But I assumed this was just temporary—until school started. It had to be.

"Okay, thanks," I said.

"Now, before I go, I need to get your tuition check," Coach said. "You do have it, right?"

I nodded. My dad had written the check, and I had stored it in the front pouch of my backpack. I pulled it out. It was made out to *Centerville Prep* in the amount of $11,000. On the bottom, my dad had written, *Jake Burnett, first-term tuition*.

"Thanks," Coach Stone said, pulling the check out of my hand. "We're happy you're here, Jake."

"Yeah," I said. "Me too."

Coach and I stepped out into the living room, where the boys were still playing *NBA 2K*. "Now, you all make Jake feel at home," he said, surveying the room.

"Coach," Thomas said. "What about food?"

"Of course," Coach Stone said. "Don't worry. I'll drop off some groceries in the morning before school. See you tomorrow, bright and early."

The boys nodded. Coach closed the front door behind him as he left. "The morning?" said a skinny black kid reclining on one of the sofas. "I'm hungry *now*."

"There's cereal and milk in there, Joey," Thomas told the boy.

Joey glanced at me as he stood up. He was about six foot six and thin, but he had the look of a serious baller. We were going to have a good team. "You hungry, man?" he asked.

"Yeah," I said. "The driver didn't show up at the airport, so I had to take the bus. Never had dinner."

The other boys exchanged quick glances before bursting into laughter. "The driver ain't never showed up," said another boy on the couch, this one a tall and stocky white kid named Dmitri.

I laughed along with the other boys. I wasn't sure what the joke was, but I was happy the ice had been broken. Joey poured me some Cheerios and I added the milk. I was starving, but I guessed the cereal would hold me until the morning.

Once I was done the Cheerios, I got up and headed back to my new bedroom. "I gotta call my parents. They worry."

I smiled. Nobody responded. They had all gone back to *2K*.

The phone rang a couple of times before Mom picked it up. "Hello!" I could hear the anticipation on the other end. She had been really worried about me making this trip alone.

"Hi, Mom," I said cheerfully. "I made it. I'm at Centerville."

"Oh, that's great," she said. "I'll get your dad on the other line."

Soon they were both talking to me. "So what's it like?" Dad asked.

"Well, I haven't seen the actual school yet because I got in so late. There was some kind of mix-up, and the driver didn't show up at the airport," I said. "But I caught a bus, and Coach Stone picked me up in Benson."

"Is everything okay though?" Mom asked. "It sounds like you had a bit of a struggle. Is your dorm good?"

"Yeah," I said, looking around the room. I was lying to her, and I didn't quite know why.

"It's fine. I met some of the guys, and our team is going to be sick!"

I spent a few more minutes on the phone with my parents before the conversation dwindled. "I guess I should probably go," I said.

"Yes, you've got your first day at your new school tomorrow," Mom said. "Better get a good sleep. And Jake..."

"Yes?"

"We miss you a ton already."

"I miss you too."

Just as I hung up, Thomas walked into the room. "Your parents?" he asked.

"Yeah," I said.

We both got ready for bed in silence. Thomas settled in with his feet going over the end of his bed and resting on top of the makeshift extension. It didn't look all that comfortable. I turned off the light and eased into my cot.

"I guess they'll probably have a proper-sized bed for you in the dorm," I said.

"Dorm?"

"Yeah, on campus at the school."

"Don't think so, man," Thomas said. "Plans might have changed a little."

I wanted to ask him what he meant by that. But after the surprises so far today, I wasn't sure I was ready for the answer. One thing was for sure though—I was tired. The cot was a little lumpy, and Thomas was already snoring. But within a few minutes, I had drifted off to sleep too.

Chapter Three

It was still dark out when I awoke. I felt my way out of the bedroom and down the narrow hallway to the bathroom. I was starving. Those Cheerios from the night before hadn't been quite enough to tide me over.

I walked past the two other bedrooms in the hallway. I was heading into the kitchen when I heard the front door open. Coach Stone burst through, a couple of white plastic bags in his hands. "Morning, Jake," he said. "Are the other guys up? School starts in less than an hour."

"No, I'm the only one awake, I think."

Coach Stone walked right past me and down the hall, banging loudly on each bedroom door as he passed it. "C'mon, boys! Time to rise and shine," he yelled. "First day of school!"

One by one, the five other boys emerged, wiping sleep from their eyes and trudging down the hallway to the bathroom. A few minutes later we were all in the kitchen with Coach Stone. The plastic bags he had carried with him were sitting on the table.

"I brought some groceries, like I promised I would," Coach said. "There's enough there for breakfast and for you guys to make some lunches. Jake, the boys can show you the way to school. Make sure you all go to the office first. I'll meet you there. Eight thirty sharp, okay?"

We all nodded. Coach Stone left through the front door. I waited for the others to begin getting their breakfast.

I was dying to eat, but I was the new kid, after all. Thomas took the lead, grabbing one grocery bag and sifting through it.

"Pop tarts, cinnamon buns, more cereal," he said.

"Milk, bread, peanut butter and jelly," added Joey, who was rifling through the other bag.

We all took turns digging in. It certainly didn't look like the breakfast buffet featured in the Centerville Prep brochure. But it was food, and I was hungry. I wolfed down a cinnamon bun and a bowl of Cheerios and made myself a peanut-butter sandwich. I grabbed another cinnamon bun for my lunch. There was no fruit or yogurt or anything remotely healthy. No lunch bags either. I put the bun and peanut-butter sandwich in the bottom of my backpack and covered them with a piece of paper towel. Luckily, I had no books in there yet.

"What time are you guys leaving for school?" I asked nobody in particular.

"We gotta go in about five," replied Thomas.

I hurried into the bathroom, washed my face, brushed my teeth and combed my hair. Maybe I could shower in the team locker room after practice.

Five minutes later I was trudging down the street with Thomas, Joey, Dmitri, Jabari and Kelvin. Thomas was the tallest of us, at six foot eleven. But we were all well over six feet except for Kelvin, a small, light-skinned black kid I guessed was probably a point guard like me. I noticed neighbors in one house peering suspiciously through their shades at us as our walking caravan made its way down the quiet street.

After a fifteen-minute walk, we arrived at a schoolyard. In the middle of a fenced field and near a large parking lot was a series of low-slung, red-brick buildings. A sign on the biggest and most central read *Theodore Roosevelt Regional High*.

"Here we are," said Dmitri. "Just gotta find the office now."

I was confused. What did Dmitri mean, *Here we are*? Where were we exactly? This wasn't a prep school. It looked like a regular public high school. There were hundreds of kids milling about on the grounds, waiting for the first bell to ring. None of them were wearing school uniforms. There was nothing on this building that said *Centerville Prep*. I wondered for a second if the guys were playing a joke on me.

"I thought we were going to Centerville Prep," I said, the words rushing out of me. "This is Roosevelt..."

Thomas turned to me, looked quickly at Dmitri and Joey, and put a hand on my shoulder. "This *is* Centerville Prep," he said. "Centerville is just the hoops part, which is sort of hosted by this school. You'll see once we actually get on the court. It's cool."

I stayed silent, just trying to absorb this latest bit of information. This wasn't how Coach Stone had sold the Centerville experience to my family and me. The brochure hadn't mentioned anything about being "hosted" by a public school. This certainly didn't look anything like the stately, ivy-covered building pictured in the promotional material.

"There's Coach," said Joey. We all walked toward Coach Stone, who was waiting outside the school's main entrance with five other boys, four of them tall and black, and one a gangly, freckled redhead.

"Hey, fellas." Coach nodded in our direction. "The other house beat y'all here. Gotta be on time for school. Just got to. Punctuality is an essential quality for any elite athlete." Thomas looked at me and rolled his eyes. Most of the other boys just nodded and lined up behind him.

We followed Coach Stone through the wide front doors of Roosevelt High and down a locker-lined hallway that led to the school office. "Coach Stone, here to see Principal Tucker," he announced to the receptionist.

She ushered him toward the principal's office. "You boys just wait here," she said, looking back at us and motioning to a row of chairs along the wall. "The coach will make sure you all get settled."

After we'd waited about twenty minutes, Coach Stone emerged with a smile on his face.

"Boys, I have a class list for each of you. It's perfect. None of you has a class ending later than 2:00 PM. I will be here at 2:15 sharp to pick you all up for practice. Don't be late." With that, Coach Stone handed us each a class schedule and was gone.

The scenario seemed weird to me, to say the least. Here I was in the middle of a school I had never heard of with a bunch of kids I had only met the night before. The school reminded me of Midland High, only bigger, older and dingier. My course list included the usual math, geography, English, chemistry and business. But it didn't include either of the optional classes I had enrolled in as part of my application to Centerville Prep. Journalism and fine arts weren't listed at all.

"Anybody got math first thing?" Kelvin asked.

"Uh, I do," I said, glancing down at my sheet.

"Good, we're together," he said, flashing a wide smile. Well, at least I wouldn't be the only new guy in the class.

"Watch out, Jake, or you gonna end up tutoring him," Thomas said with a chuckle. "Kelvin ain't exactly a rocket scientist."

Kelvin swung his backpack playfully upward. He had to jump just to hit the much taller Thomas in the shoulder. We all laughed. That helped ease the nerves a little.

Kelvin and I walked toward our first-period math class. He was about six inches shorter than me but powerfully built, with broad shoulders and thick legs resembling tree trunks. His build reminded me of Nate Robinson, the NBAer. I bet this kid could get up like Nate Robinson too. Otherwise, how could he even play?

"You nervous?" Kelvin asked.

"A little," I admitted. "This is sorta different than what I expected. I thought we'd be at a private school..."

"Don't worry, don't worry, the hoops will be good," Kelvin said. "We been ballin' a bit at the courts the last few days. Gonna be a nice team."

"That's the main thing, right?" I replied. "I mean, that's why we're here."

"I've been with Coach Stone for a while," Kelvin said. "This is, like, the third school we been at. The ball is always good, man. School is just school, you know."

I nodded. "Yeah, school is school." We headed through the door and into a crowded math class of about thirty kids. It was noisy and hot, with a lot of unfamiliar faces staring at Kelvin and me. I was glad to have at least one friend.

The rest of the day went much like the start. I found myself with Thomas for my second-period English class. At lunch we hooked up with the other basketball players, and I ate my peanut-butter sandwich and cinnamon bun. After lunch, my last class of the day was business. None of my new teammates were in the class, so I grabbed a desk at the front of the room and waited for it to begin.

A slim, brown-haired woman of about thirty-five walked into the classroom a half minute later and dropped some books on the desk at the front. "Hello, everybody."

She smiled. "For those of you who don't already know me, my name is Ms. Cuthbert, and I'll be teaching you business this semester."

Ms. Cuthbert had bright-blue eyes and an easy smile that made me feel instinctively that she was a kind person. "Let's start things off by going around the room and introducing ourselves," she said.

I hated these icebreakers, but I knew most teachers liked to use them. I guessed it saved them prep time for their first class of the year. One by one kids stood up, said their name, something interesting about themselves and whether they were new to the school. When it was my turn, I stood up slowly.

"My name is Jake Burnett," I said, feeling my cheeks flush. "I'm new. I'm from Midland, and I've moved here for my senior year to play basketball for Centerville Prep." I noticed a couple of boys lift their heads at my last sentence. They were eyeing me up and down.

"Centerville Prep?" Ms. Cuthbert said. "I haven't heard of that before. Is it a club or something?"

I couldn't believe this teacher hadn't heard of the team at her own high school. I was just about to explain about our squad when another boy in the class interjected. "That's the new prep team in town," he said. "It's part of our school this year— well, sort of anyway. I mean, we still have the Roosevelt varsity. But the players from Centerville Prep are taking classes at our school, so I guess we have two teams."

I wondered who this kid was. He seemed to know more about my new team than I did.

"Thank you, Eric," said Ms. Cuthbert. "So are you playing on the Centerville team too?"

"Nah, can't afford it," the boy said, looking down at his desk. "But I hope we play them in an exhibition or something this season. We'll kill them, for real." Eric stared at me coldly as he made this point.

I stared right back into his hard brown eyes and didn't blink. Eric looked to be about six foot four and well built. He might even be a decent basketball player. But I doubted very much he'd be "killing" anybody on our team.

I headed out to the school parking lot just after two. Coach Stone was already there, in the same minivan from the night before. Within five minutes there were eleven basketball players assembled by the open sliding door of the vehicle.

"Climb in, boys," Coach said. "You'll have to get cozy."

The van only had seating for seven, but all the boys piled in anyway. Players were sharing seats. Kelvin was basically wedged between me and the door, half-sitting on my knee. Obviously, there weren't enough seat belts to go around.

"It's only a five-minute drive, fellas," Coach said. "We'll be there before you know it."

It wasn't long before we pulled up in front of a large new silver building. This time, it was one I remembered seeing in the Centerville brochure. The sign said *Benson Recreation Center* in large white letters. Underneath, in smaller red letters, were the words *Home of Centerville Prep Basketball*.

"Y'all see the sign?" Coach said. "This is your new home. A mighty fine facility, I might add."

We followed Coach in through the double glass doors of the recreation center. We turned to the left and peered down through the windows at the gleaming hardwood below. I saw the Centerville Prep baseline logos and the growling cougar painted at midcourt. This was more like it!

Coach led us down the stairs toward a door with a sign that said *Centerville Prep Cougars*. We entered the locker room, which was lined with blond-wood bench-locker stalls. Each had an overhanging storage cupboard bearing a name on a red-and-blue nameplate. I put my backpack down underneath the nameplate *Burnett*. Unlike the house last night and the school today, this was a huge upgrade from facilities at Midland. It felt like we were in a college locker room.

"Get your gear on, boys," Coach said. "Practice starts in fifteen minutes sharp."

The first thing that hit me when I stepped onto the court wasn't how nice it was. It was very nice, but the overwhelming feeling I got was how small I suddenly seemed compared to just about everybody else out there. Starting with Thomas, all six feet eleven inches of him, through to six-foot-ten Stefan, six-foot-nine Billy, six-foot-eight Dewayne and six-foot-six Rod, this was a big, big high school squad—closer to the size of a Division 1 college team. At six foot two, I was the second-shortest player on the floor, taller only than Kelvin.

It didn't make me feel any better when, seconds after getting out there, I watched Kelvin rise effortlessly off two feet, grab an alley-oop feed from Thomas and two-hand-reverse-jam the ball through the rim. My mouth was still hanging open a second after watching this burly five-foot-eight-inch kid do something that I, a full six inches taller, couldn't come close to doing.

"Jump in there, Burnett," Coach Stone yelled in my direction. "Let's see what you got."

I was next in the warm-up line. I had barely loosened up at all, and I was nervous. I rose off the dribble and rubbed in the ball, just getting my right hand over the rim. It was a dunk, but barely. "Gotta work on those hops, Burnett," Coach said. "Gotta work on those hops."

My ears burned as I picked up the rebound and zipped the ball to the next guy in line. Great! One shot into warm-up, and already Coach Stone was pointing out my deficiencies. Still, I probably shouldn't have been surprised. My game wasn't built on pure athleticism, like it was most of these kids. I was confident I could play though.

"Okay, let's go full court one-on-one," Coach Stone said. "For you defenders, try to turn your man in the backcourt as many times as possible. Once he hits midcourt, the offensive guy can take off at full speed to the hoop. For you defenders, don't let him get there."

We all watched as the two biggest players lined up at the baseline to start the drill. Thomas had the ball, and he dribbled at about two-thirds speed, zigzagging back and forth with Stefan in a low-stance playing defense. I was impressed by how low Stefan, with his ultra-long legs, could get. And how his hands seemed to almost touch the ground when he was fully in his defensive crouch. When he reached midcourt, Thomas kicked it into another gear, pushing the ball ahead of himself and Stefan with just two speed dribbles. Stefan was quick for his size, but he couldn't catch up to Thomas's lightning strides. Thomas ran onto the ball, rose up and one-hand-tomahawked it violently through the rim. This was why Thomas Delane was being recruited by just about every major Division 1 program in the country. It was impressive.

"C'mon, Stef!" Coach Stone yelled. "You call that defense?"

I was matched up for the drill with the much smaller Kelvin. I started on defense, getting into a solid stance. Kelvin worked the ball back and forth on a string in the backcourt. I diligently stayed with him, head on the ball, using the defensive slides I had perfected at Midland. At half court, Kelvin darted right. I matched him. He darted left. I slid to match him again. But at the last second, Kelvin deftly slipped the ball through his legs and reversed directions. My feet tangled, and I fell in a heap at the free-throw line. Kelvin softly laid in the ball. The other players "oohed" playfully at his ankle-breaking move. My face flushed bright red as I got up off the floor.

"Hey, Midland, you got some work to do," Coach Stone taunted. "How you let a little guy like that cross you up so bad, Midland?"

The other players laughed—except Kelvin. He looked at me almost apologetically. I could tell he felt bad for showing me up. I hurried to the back of the line. The adjustment to prep ball was obviously going to be more difficult than I had imagined.

Not only that, but getting used to Coach Stone was also going to be an adjustment. First drill of the first practice and he had already started calling me Midland, making fun of the town I came from. I wasn't used to being the butt of a coach's joke. It didn't feel good.

The rest of the practice went a little better, but not a whole lot. I seemed constantly a step behind most of the other kids, particularly Thomas, Kelvin, Stef and Joey. They were clearly Coach Stone's favorites, and for good reason. They were really, really good. Each one of them was athletic, skilled and tough. They led all the drills and were near perfect at them in just our first practice.

The whistle finally sounded at 5:00 PM. We had already been practicing for two and a half hours, and I was exhausted. Coach Stone called us to the middle of the court. "Well, fellas, that was a pretty good effort for our first real practice," he said. "But some of you have some serious work to do." Maybe I was imagining it, but Coach seemed to be looking straight at me.

41

"Some of you have some adjustments to make in order to play minutes at this level."

I gulped, looking around at the talented cast of basketball players gathered on the court. This was a different feeling for me. I had always been at least one of the best, if not the very best, player on the floor. Suddenly, here, I was middle of the pack or worse. The only kid I was absolutely certain I was better than was Billy, the gangly forward from Texas with the bright-red hair and freckles. He was pretty uncoordinated, but at least he was six foot nine. I was only six two and obviously not as athletic as half the kids out here. Was I really ready for this?

"We'll have an intrasquad scrimmage tomorrow," Coach Stone continued. "By the time you leave today, I'll have rosters for that scrimmage posted outside the locker-room door. You'll either be on the Red or the White team for tomorrow. That scrimmage will get us ready for our first real game—here—against Stanton Prep on Wednesday."

Our first game? Only two days after our first practice? Was Coach kidding? We hadn't even discussed offensive or defensive schemes yet. I hadn't played a minute of real basketball with any of these kids. At Midland, we had practiced for three solid weeks before we played our first exhibition game. This seemed bizarre.

We filed into the locker room, most of the guys joking around and talking. I didn't feel much like making jokes though. It had been a frustrating and humiliating practice. I hadn't done anything very well. Coach Stone had been on me from the warm-up. It hadn't been all that encouraging or even much fun.

"Told you the ball was good," Kelvin said as he slid into the locker stall beside mine.

"Yeah, it is. I sucked out there though," I said quietly.

"Don't worry—it will get better." He smiled. "You gotta remember that most of us have been together for a while. You're new. It might take some time."

I nodded. Kelvin's words made me feel a little better. I decided not to jump to any conclusions that day. The gym and the locker-room facility were top-notch, and the level of basketball was obviously terrific. It was simple. I would just have to get better.

Chapter Four

"What did I tell ya? Franks and beans," Thomas yelled from the kitchen.

"Not again!" moaned Joey. "How many times is that already?"

Nobody bothered to answer.

I walked into the kitchen after dropping off my backpack in the bedroom. Joey and Thomas were already starting to prepare supper. Thomas was opening a third can of baked beans while Joey cut up a dozen wieners. Dmitri was making toast.

"This," Thomas said, "is dinner."

I grabbed six glasses from the kitchen cupboard. "Everybody want milk?" I asked. All heads nodded. I filled each glass and placed them on the table. In minutes, we were eating wieners and beans and toast and talking about our first day at school and practice.

"It's okay, I guess," Thomas said. "My teachers seem pretty chill, and besides, who cares about school? I'm going to the association." With that, he grabbed a hunk of paper towel from beside his plate and reverse-dunked it into the big black garbage can that sat in the corner of the kitchen.

"It's better than the last school," Kelvin said. "That place was lame. It wasn't even really a school. At least this one has other kids in it. And teachers."

"What other school?" I asked. "I thought Centerville Prep has been going for a while now."

"Centerville is basically just Coach Stone," Thomas explained. "Me, Kelvin, Stef and Joey—we been with Coach for three years now. First year was in Kentucky, second year Kansas. Now we're here in Benson. It don't matter where the school is, it's how good the ball is. If you play good ball, the colleges will take notice. Least, that's what Coach says."

This was news to me. Coach Stone hadn't mentioned that the Centerville Prep program had been moved around during the last three years. I'd just assumed it had always been here in Benson. But that explained why Thomas, Kelvin, Stef and Joey seemed to know what to do in practice. They had been playing with Coach for a while. They were tight with him.

I had found it strange when I looked at the lineups for the next day's scrimmage that those four had been placed on the Red team, along with Jabari and Ricky, a player who lived at the other house. I was one of five kids on the White team and, from what I could remember from practice, our lineup was considerably weaker than the Red team. It was going to be an interesting scrimmage.

We all pitched in to clean up after dinner. Then, one by one, we ended up in the living room on the two leather sofas, taking turns playing *NBA 2K*. I played with the Toronto Raptors and used Kyle Lowry to near perfection as I beat each one of the other kids. I was king of *2K* for the night.

"Nice job, Midland," cracked Dmitri after we were done. "At least you can play the game on the screen." Everybody laughed, including me, but after the day I'd had, I was stinging a little as I went to bed.

"Hey, man, don't let it get you down," Thomas said through the darkness as we lay in our beds. "Coach is always a little hard on the new guys. It'll get better—you'll see."

Thomas's words were still floating around in my head as I drifted off to sleep. I hoped the big fella was right.

Even though day one at practice hadn't gone as I'd hoped, the competitor inside me could hardly wait for the second day of school to begin. I was excited about the scrimmage Coach Stone had set up for that afternoon. I was determined to make my mark in that session. To show Coach what I could do and earn some playing time for our first game against Stanton Prep the following day.

I just hoped I would have enough energy for the game. On my second morning in the house, there had been only bread, peanut butter and jelly available for lunches. I had slapped together two sandwiches, but that was all I could find to pack. I had been hoping to find a vending machine at school to pick up another snack, but I hadn't seen one yet as I headed into business, my final class of the day. My stomach was already grumbling, but I guessed I could survive until dinner.

Ms. Cuthbert started off the class with a question. She wrote it on the blackboard: *What is a contract?*

"Anybody?" she asked, surveying the room. Eric, the kid who had spoken out the day before about Centerville Prep, shot up his hand. "It's when two parties agree on a deal of some kind," he said.

"Correct," Ms. Cuthbert said. "Does anybody care to elaborate?"

A girl named Crystal, sitting two rows away from me, stuck up a hand. "Well, usually one person who is part of the contract is providing a service or some goods or something, and the other is buying those services or goods."

"Again, correct," Ms. Cuthbert said. "A big part of this business class will be studying contracts and the relationships involved in those contracts—between the supplier and the purchaser."

I was actually interested in this subject, unlike math. My uncle Steve worked as a contract lawyer. He was involved in making big-time business deals in Chicago. I had always thought that was an interesting career. Maybe something I'd like to try after college and, I hoped, my pro-basketball days.

"The biggest thing about a contract is that it is a formal agreement," Ms. Cuthbert continued. "Let's say Jake here promises that he will provide me with a service. Then let's say the service doesn't live up to how he described it when he sold it to me. In that case, he has violated our contract—he hasn't lived up to our agreement. In this class we'll learn, among other things, what happens in these cases and how the precise wording of contracts is very important in order to ensure that both parties in a deal are protected."

I chuckled to myself. Coach Stone was a service provider who had sold my family and me on a pretty nice description of Centerville Prep. Good thing nobody was checking up on whether he had fulfilled the details of his contract.

All thoughts of contracts and suppliers and business had disappeared from my thoughts by the time Coach Stone arrived to pick us up for practice at 2:15 PM. Once again we crowded into his minivan, like a pack of clowns at a circus. I wondered what would happen if the police ever pulled Coach over. Seven seat belts for eleven players didn't quite add up.

When we got to the rec center, Coach Stone pulled us together in the parking lot. He handed out red Centerville Prep practice jerseys to Thomas, Kelvin, Stef, Joey, Jabari and Ricky. He handed out whites to Dmitri, Dewayne, Rod, Billy and me. "Suit up and warm up," Coach said. "Scrimmage will begin at 3:00 PM sharp."

Once out on the court, I surveyed the lineups for this scrimmage. The Reds had the two tallest players on the team—six-foot-eleven Thomas and six-foot-ten Stef. They had probably the best outside shooters in wings Joey and Jabari, each about six foot six, and a six-foot-four sinewy defensive stopper in Ricky. They also had Kelvin, who, even though he was the shortest kid on the team, was likely the best pure athlete. They would be a load for us to play against.

Meanwhile, on the White team, we had decent size with six-foot-eight Dewayne and six-foot-nine Billy, though neither was close to being as mobile or explosive as Thomas, or as tough as Stef. Dmitri and Rod were both solidly-built kids of about six foot six, and both were new to the team like me. We had no subs.

Coach Stone's whistle blew, and we lined up at midcourt for the opening tip. "I will be the referee," Coach said, "and my calls are final. No whining."

Coach Stone tossed the ball high in the air for the tip. Thomas easily outjumped Dewayne to tip the ball back toward Kelvin in the Red team's backcourt. But I had been anticipating that we would lose the jump, and I was moving toward the ball before Kelvin. I stole the tip, crossed my dribble over to the left and took off hard for the layup—or, at least, what I thought would be a layup. Just as I was about to flip the ball from my left hand onto the backboard, Thomas's long right arm shot over top of me. Not only did he block my shot, but he actually pinned the ball to the backboard before coming down with the rebound in one hand.

"Gotta score that, Jake!" Coach Stone yelled. Terrific. Six seconds into the scrimmage, and I had already made my first mistake.

As I had expected, the Reds dominated from that moment on. Coach had put twenty minutes of running time up on the clock, and by the time it had wound down, the Reds were leading 44–15. They had fed the smooth-shooting Thomas at every opportunity, and he had responded with what had seemed liked thirty of their forty-four points.

On the bright side, I had hit one deep three from the corner and a pair of free throws after drawing a foul from Kelvin on a nice pump fake. Meanwhile, I had done a decent job defending Kelvin. He had trouble scoring over me due to the height differential between us, but he had managed one fast-break dunk after he leaked out and took a bullet pass from Thomas.

While we all took a water break at half-time, Rod asked Coach Stone what everybody on our team had been thinking. "Coach, how about mixing up the teams a little?" said the lanky shooter with the unmistakable Louisiana twang in his voice. "The Reds are pretty strong."

"We'll leave it the way it is," replied Coach, dismissing the suggestion. "The Reds are basically our starters. I want to give them as many minutes together today as possible so that they'll be ready for tomorrow."

Our starters? I wondered how Coach Stone had already decided who the starters for our team were going to be. We'd had only one practice and this scrimmage. It wasn't that I disagreed necessarily that the Reds were our best players. It was just that there had been no process.

Rod didn't respond to Coach's answer. None of us on the White team did. But as the Reds took the ball out of bounds to start the second half, I could sense that the kids on my team were pissed. None of us had left our homes, our families, our friends and our schools to be labeled right away as backups. We were going to play the second half as though we had something to prove.

Maybe that's what Coach had been after when he made up these teams for the scrimmage. I went into a defensive stance to guard Kelvin, who was bringing the ball upcourt. Maybe Coach wanted to see what kind of character some of his "new" kids possessed.

Whatever the reason, the second half of the scrimmage was a lot more intense. The Reds had come out on fire in the first half, particularly after Thomas's big swat on me to open the game. They were playing with a little less of an edge in the second half, and we were upping our intensity. After three White steals and lay-ins on the first six Red possessions of the half—two of them by me stripping Kelvin—Coach Stone angrily blew his whistle. It was now 46–24 and becoming much more competitive.

"That's it! Scrimmage is over!" Coach yelled. "Both teams get on the baseline." I knew this wouldn't be good. *Get on the baseline* was basketball-coach code for "I'm going to run you guys till you drop."

"You guys stopped working hard," Coach continued to fume. "And if you're not going to work, then you're going to run—without any basketballs."

I groaned. The White team certainly hadn't stopped working. We had actually played a lot harder in the second half. But Coach seemed extremely disappointed that the Red team hadn't continued to dominate us.

"We're doing man-makers," Coach Stone announced. Whatever a coach called them—man-makers, suicides, shuttles—they were difficult. Players had to run from baseline to foul line and back, then to center line and back, to the far foul line and back, and, finally, to the far baseline and back. At each of those points we had to bend down and touch the gym floor. Doing one of those sequences was fine. But if you had to do multiple man-makers, it was exhausting.

"We're doing five man-makers," Coach announced. "But for every one not completed in under thirty-five seconds, we'll do two more."

All of us grimaced. It would be tough for the big kids to keep up to that pace.

Sure enough, three man-makers in, Dewayne didn't make the thirty-five-second limit. "That's two extra for everybody," Coach yelled.

Everybody groaned. Joey scowled at Dewayne. "C'mon man!" he said. "We don't want to be here all night."

Dewayne chugged out the next two man-makers in time. But on the final one, he was again a half second slow crossing the line. So was Rod. This time, nobody said anything.

"Two more," Coach said.

"Let's go, fellas!" Thomas yelled as we took off in a group. Something encouraging in his voice seemed to pick everybody up. Rod and Dewayne dug deep, and everybody crossed the baseline for the final man-maker within the time limit. Not without some drama, however. Billy immediately rushed to the big green trash bin near the gym door and threw up in it. The rest of us stared as the redhead retched uncontrollably.

"Maybe next time, y'all will play with intensity," Coach Stone said. "Either that or we can do man-makers all day. Up to you guys."

As I headed to the locker room with the rest of the guys, I was thinking that Coach was wrong. It wasn't up to us—at least, not to the White team. It was up to Coach's stars. That was all he seemed to care about anyway.

Chapter Five

I was finding it difficult to do my math homework. Not that the math itself was hard—actually, it was just review of work that I had covered in my last school year at Midland. But the only place for me to do it with any sort of privacy was sitting on my bed, which made it difficult to write neatly. I didn't have the luxury of my desk back at home. Making it even tougher was the fact that I was preoccupied with the way the scrimmage had gone that afternoon and how Coach Stone was so obviously playing favorites.

The "Sweet Georgia Brown" ringtone of my cell phone interrupted my thoughts. I had picked that ringtone after seeing the Harlem Globetrotters play a couple of years back, but now it seemed sort of juvenile.

"Hello?"

"Hi, Jake!" It was Mom.

"Hi, son!" Dad chimed in, likely from the phone in their bedroom.

We had agreed to talk two nights into my stay at Centerville, but I had forgotten about it. It was good to hear their voices. I'd never thought I would actually miss home. But if I was being honest with myself, I was already homesick. At least, a little.

"How's everything going?" Mom said, her voice rising slightly in a way that seemed a little anxious. "Did you get all your classes arranged okay? How's your dorm room? Is everything as nice as it looked in the pictures?"

"It's great," I said, not really addressing her questions. "The guys are pretty cool, and my teachers seem fine. And you should see our home court. It is awesome. I even have a nameplate on my locker stall. Just like the big time."

I didn't really understand why I was selling them so hard on how good it was here at Centerville. But I felt like that's what I had to do—what they wanted to hear. I had worked so hard on coaxing them to let me come here, and they had agreed to pay a lot of money—more than $20,000—in tuition and boarding fees to send me. I didn't have the heart to tell them that I was actually attending class in a public school. Or that my "dorm" was this crappy house we were all sharing without any real supervision or even decent food.

"Are they feeding you good, Jake?" Mom asked. "As good as my cooking?" She laughed.

"No, not as good as your cooking," I replied. At least I wasn't lying about that. We'd had wieners and beans for the second straight night. And so far there never seemed to be quite enough food for six growing athletes. "But it's okay. I'll survive."

"How is that journalism class?" asked Dad. "You seemed pretty excited about taking that. Is that something you think you might be interested in for college?"

"Yeah, maybe," I said, sidestepping the actual question. There was no journalism class. No fine arts either. In fact, I was only taking five classes. But how could I tell them that?

"The team is really good," I continued. "We've got our first game tomorrow against Stanton, and I think we're going to start the year in the National Prep Top 20."

"Wow," Dad said. "Pretty impressive. Just remember, though, school comes first. I'm okay with this basketball focus, but you need your grades for college. A scholarship is no good if you can't even get into a school."

"Yes, Dad, I know," I said. "Don't worry, I'm working hard."

After exchanging some more small talk about the weather and a movie Mom and

Dad had gone to watch the night before, I cut them off. "I better get going," I said. "I've got quite a bit of homework to do, and we've got a game tomorrow...I can call you on the weekend."

"Okay, Jake," Mom said. "We miss you."

"I miss you too."

I felt bad after hanging up. I wasn't really all that anxious to get back to my homework. But talking with my parents had begun to make me feel uncomfortable. I hadn't really lied to them, but I hadn't really told them the truth either. I lay back on my bed. It was early, but I just wanted to go to sleep now. It had been a long couple of days.

Despite my concerns about lying to Mom and Dad, I was pumped for our first game against Stanton. It was hard to believe we were already playing a real game, with just one practice and one scrimmage under our belts.

I slogged my way through the school day, daydreaming about the game and visualizing how I was going to play—tough, smart, cool with the ball and deadly from behind the three-point line. It was going to be a dream lining up alongside Thomas and some of these other kids. I had never actually thrown an alley-oop in a real game. I wondered if it would happen today.

Coach picked us up from Roosevelt after our last class as usual and drove us to the Benson Recreation Center for a walk-through and afternoon shoot-around. Game time wasn't until 7:00 PM, so after the shoot-around he drove us to the Metro Diner, about a mile away from the rec center. We got out of the van, dressed in our red-and-blue team warm-ups, and filed into the upscale steakhouse. The manager of the restaurant greeted Coach at the door with a big smile and a handshake.

"Welcome to the Metro," he said to each of us as we were seated at a table for twelve. "Coach Stone has preordered for you, and we'll have your meals to you shortly." In no time, a waiter was bringing out our plates—roasted chicken breast, green salad and vegetables. The food looked as appealing as any meal I could remember. I glanced around the table as all the players began chowing down with Coach. This was great! There had been a few bumps so far at Centerville, sure, but this pregame meal was awesome. I felt just like an NBAer.

When we had finished, Coach ushered us out of the restaurant and back into the van. We drove the few minutes back to the rec center. As we climbed out of the crowded vehicle, Coach handed each of us a white jersey and a pair of matching shorts. My jersey bore a red number *10* on both the back and front and my name, *Burnett*, in red letters across the back. I was jacked to be able to finally slip on this uniform and get out on the court for a real game.

A few minutes later, we were all dressed in our new home Centerville whites, complete with the custom socks Coach had provided with the Cougars logo on the back of the ankle. We looked more like a pro team than a prep squad. With all the size and basketball talent in this room, I was feeling invincible.

Coach Stone entered the locker room and cleared his throat. "Listen up, fellas," he said. "I have great hopes for you this season. I hope you are dreaming big too. I believe that in this room we have the talent to win a national prep title."

I could feel tingles running through my body. Coach's words were inspiring me. I scanned the faces of the other guys in the room. We were all business.

"What remains to be seen is whether we have the desire, the toughness and the commitment to be that good," Coach Stone continued. "We can start proving that tonight on the court against Stanton. Now let's get out there and tear them up!"

The team exploded out of the locker room and onto the court. I was surprised to see that with still nearly a half hour till tip-off, there were already a few hundred fans in the stands. There were even a couple of reporters at the media table that ran along the court opposite the benches and the scorekeepers' table. This was certainly a lot different than games at old Midland High.

Coach had already gone over some basics about Stanton. They had a pretty decent big man in Keith Jones, a six-foot-ten senior. Jones was not overly strong for his size inside but was a deadly three-point shooter. It would be a showdown between him and Thomas. Thomas was an inch taller and far more athletic. He was more a quintessential North American big man while Jones was more in the European mold.

Coach had also already announced our starting lineup. I hadn't been overly surprised not to be included, but it still hurt. This would be the first high-school game I'd ever begun on the bench, and it felt weird. But I was confident I could contribute to what I hoped would be a convincing Centerville victory.

Our starters—Thomas, Kelvin, Stef, Joey and Jabari—were seated on the bench as Coach Stone faced them in the pregame huddle.

The rest of the team, me included, stood behind and around Coach. The stands behind us and on the other side of the court were now almost full. There must have been close to a thousand people in the gym, and you could feel their heat and energy.

"Okay, fellas," Coach said. "We need a big start here. We're in a 2-3 zone on D and we're running high screen with Thomas and Kelvin to start on offense. Okay?" All heads nodded.

Thomas easily beat Jones to win the opening tip, rising above his adversary to bat the ball back to Kelvin. He then sauntered downcourt and set a high screen just below the three-point line, near the right elbow of the foul line. Kelvin calmly worked his man toward the screen, faked left and then dribbled right, hard around Thomas. Jones switched out to pick up Kelvin. Kelvin deftly slipped the ball back to Thomas on the classic pick-and-roll, and Thomas finished with a thundering dunk inside. Stanton's point guard didn't have a hope of stopping him. We were up 2-0, just like that.

And that is pretty much how the entire first half went. Kelvin and Thomas ran the two-man game to perfection, with either Thomas finishing strong inside or Kelvin nailing a jumper, while Stef slid to the opposite block and collected rebounds, and Joey and Jabari spotted up to shoot threes. On defense, Thomas anchored our zone in the middle and discouraged anybody from coming too close. With three minutes left in the half, we were already up twenty-five points.

Coach looked down the bench. My stomach flipped. I hoped he was looking for subs. "Dewayne, Dmitri," Coach barked. "Go in for Thomas and Stef." My heart sank. I would have to wait a little longer, I guessed. Coach was subbing forwards now—guards would hopefully happen soon.

Those were the only subs Coach made before the half, however. By now we were up thirty on Stanton, at 51-21. This was no longer even a game. As we filed into the locker room for halftime, we were joking around about how easy the first twenty minutes had been.

That didn't last long.

"I don't know what you all are laughing about!" Coach Stone screamed at us, his eyes bulging. Everybody in the room, including me, was taken aback. "You haven't proved nothin' to me yet. This is a team we should beat by eighty. But in the last few minutes of that half, you were soft and lazy. Nobody took a charge out there. Nobody was in a stance. We got out-rebounded by them in the final two minutes. The game shouldn't be anywhere near this close. If you don't want to play, just tell me now, and I'll get you off the court!"

Nobody said a word. I was dumbfounded. After Coach stormed out of the locker room, I whispered to a very sweaty Kelvin, who was sitting beside me, "What would he be like if we were losing?"

Kelvin shook his head. "That's just Coach. He's never satisfied. You'll get used to it."

I didn't know what to say. I guess it might have been easier to listen to if I'd actually got on the court in the first half. It was irritating to hear Coach talk about taking guys off if they didn't want to play. I *wanted* to play! Sitting on the bench was a new experience for me, and one I wasn't enjoying at all. Maybe Coach would be pissed enough to put out a whole new starting five for the second half.

Those thoughts were dashed when Coach gathered us after the break. "Original starters down," he said tersely. Thomas, Kelvin, Stef, Joey and Jabari plopped down in front of him. "Now show me," Coach said slowly, "that you can play dominating basketball."

Dominating was a good description of how the guys looked during the next ten minutes, running at will, stealing the ball, nailing threes and throwing down dunks. By the end of the third quarter, the score had ballooned to 77–32. I looked down the bench at Coach. Our starters had played the entire third quarter. Surely he would put in some subs now, wouldn't he?

"Dmitri, Dewayne, you're in," Coach said, motioning to the two players. Thomas and Kelvin moved off their chairs, and Dmitri and Dewayne took their places with the rest of the starters. I wasn't sure how Thomas and Kelvin knew they were being subbed out. Meanwhile, Coach still wasn't calling my name. What was going on here?

The fourth quarter rolled ahead, with the slaughter continuing. With three minutes left, we were up 89-45. We now had a forty-four-point lead. Stanton had given up, with its entire bench now in the game, yet Billy and I still hadn't been on the floor. Billy looked as miserable as I felt inside, his head resting on his palm as he stared out at the court. I glanced down the bench, and my eyes met Coach Stone's. He looked right through me.

Still no call to sub.

When the final horn sounded, our Centerville squad had won 100-52. Stef had broken the century mark for us with a vicious reverse slam that had brought everybody, including me, off the bench, waving our towels. Still, as we headed into the locker room, I didn't feel good at all. I was confused. Why hadn't I got into the game? I hadn't expected to start—at least, not this early in the season—but to get zero minutes in a massive blowout was shocking and embarrassing.

I dressed slowly and was the last guy left in the locker room when Coach Stone stuck his head in the door. "Let's go, Burnett!" he said curtly. "The van is leaving!"

I figured I didn't have anything to lose at that point, and the words just came tumbling out. "Coach, why didn't I get in tonight?" I said, trying to make it sound like a casual question and not like I was whining.

Coach Stone looked at me sternly and shook his head. "You got to earn your minutes, Burnett," he said, not a trace of compassion in his voice. "I haven't seen anything from you yet that has earned you any minutes."

Was this guy kidding? We had only had one practice and one scrimmage, in which he had drawn up completely lopsided teams.

What chance had I actually been given to earn my minutes or show Coach anything? I was so shocked at what he had said, I couldn't think of any response.

"I play an eight-man rotation," Coach continued. "If you're not part of it, you have to do whatever it takes to help the team, be it in practice or whatever."

I could feel the tears welling up inside me. I was furious. I followed Coach out to the van and jammed myself into the vehicle that would take us home. The guys were hooting and hollering and celebrating the big win. Celebrating was the last thing I felt like doing.

Minutes after Coach dropped us off at the house, the guys were already in the kitchen, rustling up peanut-butter-and-jelly sandwiches. I wasn't hungry. I was angry. Coach's words about contributing in other ways if I wasn't in his top eight still stung. How did that work? I hadn't come all the way to Centerville to be a benchwarmer.

Kelvin eyed me carefully as I sat in a chair at the kitchen table, not eating and hardly talking. "Hey, man," he said quietly. "Don't worry, you'll get some minutes. Coach just knows Thomas and me and a few of the other kids. He's comfortable with us. We've been playing AAU for him since we were nine."

I nodded sullenly. I knew Kelvin was trying to make me feel better, but it wasn't working. It seemed like Coach had made up his mind about me pretty quickly, and I wasn't in his rotation. "Maybe," I said. "That was a new thing for me tonight though. I never went a whole game without playing before."

The guys all piled into the living room to play *2K*, but once again I just felt tired. The day had started great. I had been so excited about the game and our uniforms and the big-time atmosphere in the gym. But not getting in, even when we were absolutely crushing our opponents, had left me upset and confused and completely drained. I quietly slipped off to bed. Maybe tomorrow would be better. I sure hoped so.

Chapter Six

I had made an appointment to see Ms. Munoz, the school's academic counselor, at 10:00 AM the next day. So after my first class of the morning, I found her office in the administration wing of Roosevelt and knocked on the door.

"Come on in," said the warm voice from inside. I opened the door to the smile of a tall woman who looked to be in her mid-forties. She had long dark hair tied back in a ponytail.

Unlike other counselors and teachers, Ms. Munoz was dressed casually in a Roosevelt Roughriders basketball sweat suit. It was green and white, the colors of the high school I was actually attending but not playing for. That part still seemed weird.

"Hi," she said. "You must be Jake. Welcome. What can I do for you today?"

Ms. Munoz flipped open a file folder on her desk. I guessed all my information was in it. "I see here that you're quite a basketball player," she said. "On the Centerville Prep team! Very impressive. I know you have to be pretty good to play on that squad."

"I guess," I said, somewhat embarrassed. What I was really thinking was, I wouldn't know, because I haven't actually played yet for Centerville—just sat on the bench.

"Your files show that you're a senior, a transfer from Midland High. Are you hoping to graduate this year, Jake?"

What did she mean, *hoping*? Of course I was going to graduate.

"The reason I ask is that you're only enrolled in five classes," she said. "You need another two class credits to have enough to graduate. Is there a reason you haven't enrolled in two more?"

I hadn't even thought about that until now. I felt so stupid. I was supposed to be taking journalism and fine arts too. At least, that's what I had requested on my application to Centerville Prep.

"I signed up for journalism when I applied to Centerville," I explained. "And fine arts too. But I didn't see those classes on the schedule that I got the first day here. That's actually what I wanted to talk to you about today."

Ms. Munoz looked confused. "Well, I wish we had a journalism program to offer you, Jake, but we don't," she said gently. "And we have a ceramics class or a photography class that you could take, but there is no fine arts course per se."

I wasn't all that surprised. Not much about the academic side of things here was quite as Coach Stone had described. I was just lucky I had decided to see Ms. Munoz this morning. What if I'd gone through a couple of months of school without checking into it? How would my parents have reacted if they had spent more than $20,000 on a prep school and I didn't even graduate?

"The photography sounds good," I said. "Is there some other elective I can take instead of journalism?"

"I can still get you into our creative-writing course, I think," Ms. Munoz said. "However, this note in your file says that you are not supposed to take a course that ends after 2:15 PM. Creative writing goes until 3:00 every Monday afternoon. Would your coach be okay with that?"

"I can ask," I said. "Thanks."

"Well, let me know before Monday, if possible," Ms. Munoz said. "We need to get on this quickly."

I nodded in agreement. I grabbed my backpack and prepared to leave for my next class.

"Can I ask you a question before you go, Jake?" she said.

"Sure."

"Did Coach Stone tell you that you would be able to take journalism and fine arts here at Roosevelt?"

"There was a list of courses to choose from," I said, recalling the Centerville brochure. I had been so pumped about coming to the team that I had just about memorized the entire contents of that document. "There were a bunch of languages, robotics, scuba diving—stuff like that."

"I see," Ms. Munoz said. "And do you mind my asking what kind of fees your parents are paying for you to be in the Centerville Prep program?"

"I think about $22,000 for the whole year," I said. "Maybe some other registration costs too."

Ms. Munoz rolled her eyes. "Okay, thanks, Jake," she said. "Come see me again before Monday."

As I left her office, I wondered why she had asked me those questions about Centerville Prep. But I was more concerned with what Coach Stone was going to say when I asked him my question that after-noon. Would he be okay with me not getting to practice until later on Mondays? He would have to be. I didn't see what other choice I had.

Coach Stone picked us up as usual for Thursday afternoon's practice. I was expecting a tough one. We had our second game coming up on Saturday evening. It was a home contest against Skyline Prep—a National Top 10 team from out of state. Coach would want us to be in top form for that one. I just hoped we could concentrate on basketball enough to avoid doing man-makers this time.

I knew the only time I would get to ask Coach about the creative-writing course was before practice. So after the other guys had disappeared into the locker room to change, I found him sitting in the bleachers of the empty gym. He raised his eyebrows as I approached him, like he was surprised I wasn't getting ready for practice.

"Coach, I need to ask you something," I said.

"Go ahead," Coach Stone said. "What is it?"

I was nervous, so I started rambling about why I would need to be late for every Monday practice. How I needed to add another course and creative writing was as close to the journalism course I had signed up for as Roosevelt could offer. I expected him to offer some sort of explanation for why the courses his Centerville brochure had advertised weren't actually available. I was wrong.

"Why are you bothering me with this non-basketball stuff, Burnett?" he said brusquely. "If you need another course, just take one that doesn't go past 2:15. That's when the van leaves the school for practice."

"But I need a writing course if I want to get into journalism in college," I said. "You told me when I applied to Centerville Prep that you offered a journalism course—"

Coach Stone interrupted me. "And you told me that you were a college-level athlete," he shot back. "From what I've seen so far, that's a stretch."

I was shocked by Coach's comment. I had never said I was a college-level player. In fact, he was the one who had told me he thought I could play college basketball. His comment was unexpectedly vicious, and it hurt. So this was what he really thought of me.

"I'll tell you what," he continued. "Take your creative-writing course. I don't care. But you'll have to find your own way to practice on Mondays. I'm not making two trips. I don't run no bus service."

I was silent. Coach's attitude floored me. I didn't know how to respond.

"Now get going and get ready for practice," he growled. "Starts in five minutes."

I headed back to the locker room, feeling more dejected than I could ever remember feeling. I settled in quietly beside Kelvin, who was busy putting new laces in his high-top Jordans.

"Where you been?" Kelvin said. "Practice is starting real soon."

"Just forgot something in the van," I said. "Had to get Coach to open it up for me."

Once again, I was lying. I didn't want my teammates to know about the discussion I'd just had with Coach Stone. Not even Kelvin.

Despite the terrible interaction with Coach, practice that day went pretty well. I was on fire from outside, hitting two deep threes during the session-ending scrimmage and keeping Kelvin in check. During the twenty-minute game, I kept him in front of me and off the scoreboard. Our over-matched White team lost to the Reds again, but this time only by a 30–20 margin. And, strangely enough, Coach Stone wasn't mad this time as he gathered us at midcourt at the end of the two-and-a half-hour practice.

"Great job today, boys," Coach said. "Skyline is a huge challenge for us. Kyle Winston is a terrific guard—maybe the best in the whole country. But I know we can handle him and get a win. As long as everyone brings his A game."

Inside I groaned as I listened to Coach's words. It didn't matter what game I brought if I didn't get off the bench. But after the way I'd guarded Kelvin today, and after shooting the way I did, Coach had to play me, didn't he?

Chapter Seven

By the time Saturday evening rolled around, I had convinced myself that the Skyline game was going to be different. I would get some minutes and contribute and show Coach Stone that I was more than capable of helping the team. It didn't hurt my mood that it had been a glorious, sunny fall day in Benson and the guys and I had walked to the Metro Diner for our pregame meal. The atmosphere was light and confident as we ate and then headed to Benson Rec Center with Coach.

A couple of hours later, we were warming up in an already-packed gym. As I stretched at center court, I watched as Skyline, in its powder-blue-and-silver uniforms, went through its pregame rituals. Kyle Winston, Skyline's six-foot-five McDonald's High School All-American, was taking pass after pass on the baseline from an assistant coach. I was counting his three-point makes. At twenty in a row, I stopped counting and concentrated on my own stretching. Winston was an amazing knock-down shooter. I badly wanted a chance to guard him that night.

Once again, however, I was not in the Centerville starting lineup. The top five were identical to what they had been since our first practice. And Coach didn't make a single sub during the entire first quarter. At the end of that eight-minute period, we were up 16–14. But Winston had nailed three three-pointers, all on Kelvin's head. Kelvin was just too short to be able to bother the Skyline shooter's smooth release to any degree.

"Thomas," Coach said during the huddle, "I want you to switch onto Winston. Get a hand up in his face. His looks have been way too easy."

Thomas nodded. I checked the reaction on Kelvin's face. He wasn't happy. Basically, Coach had just told the entire team that Kelvin had done a poor job of defending Winston. When we broke our huddle, the whole gym would know. But the change with Thomas and Kelvin meant everybody else's defensive assignment was changed as well. Moving Thomas on to Kyle Winston was a bit of gamble. It meant that Kelvin ended up covering Tatum Rice, Skyline's silky-smooth, six-foot-six forward. That was a huge mismatch too. I couldn't help but think Coach should be putting me in the game. Kelvin was certainly more athletic, but I was longer and stronger. I would be capable of staying on either Winston or Rice.

Coach didn't make a single sub in the second quarter either. I could tell that all the guys on the bench were getting antsy. Dewayne was overtly angry, throwing a towel down in disgust after a timeout ended and he still remained on the bench. But what did Dewayne have to complain about? At least he'd actually been in a game. I glanced over at Billy, who, like me, had yet to play a minute. He was again sitting glumly at the end of the bench. His heavily freckled face looked disengaged, like he had given up any hope of seeing the floor this season. I, on the other hand, wasn't ready to surrender to Coach Stone.

The half ended with us up 45-35. The second quarter had gone much better. Thomas had poured in fifteen points and held Winston scoreless as we increased our lead. But Skyline was staying in the game by going to Tatum Rice, who was taking the much smaller Kelvin down to the block and posting him up for easy hook shots. Rice had thirteen points in the quarter.

"Kelvin, can you guard anybody today?" Coach yelled in the locker room during the intermission. Sitting right beside Kelvin,

I could feel the spit flying from Coach Stone's lips as he chewed out our tiny point guard. Even though I believed I should have been playing in this game ahead of Kelvin, I felt bad for the kid.

Coach was generally happy with the way the team had played in the first half, though, and why not? Skyline was ranked number 6 in the entire country. We were number 15. If our lead held up, it would be considered a major upset, and we'd rise in the rankings. I thought I noticed an extra swagger in Coach's step as he left the locker room. One by one, we got up and followed him out onto the court for the second half.

I decided to make a move. I hustled a few steps ahead of my teammates and caught up to Coach.

"Coach Stone, I can guard Winston," I said. It wasn't a boast. I was confident I could do just that.

He didn't even look my way. "I make the decisions," he hissed under his breath. "Never, *ever* talk to me during a game about playing time! You understand?"

I could tell by the harshness in Coach's voice that I better not push it any further. I settled onto the bench for the start of the second half wondering if I had just made a huge tactical error.

Thomas continued on his personal tear once the second half started, scoring fourteen more in the third quarter, including two posterizing dunks on Winston that had the crowd going crazy. By the end of the quarter, we were up twenty and running away with it. Finally, Coach looked down his bench. He had not made a single sub up to this point. I found that incredible. "Dewayne, Dmitri," he barked. "Let's go—for Stef and Kelvin."

And that was it. Kelvin went directly to the end of the bench. He'd had a terrible game. Five points, one rebound and a porous defensive effort that had seen him absolutely abused by first Winston and then Rice. But any hope I had harbored of going in for Kelvin was dashed when Coach subbed in Dmitri. Or maybe it had disappeared when I decided to talk to Coach at halftime.

Regardless, when the final horn sounded, we had won 102–80 and, once again, I had failed to get off the bench.

The great mood I had been in before Saturday's game was long gone by Sunday morning. After a week at Centerville, I was seriously second-guessing my choice to come here. I wasn't playing. I wasn't taking what I wanted to in school. I had a lousy relationship with Coach, and the food at our house was terrible. I was homesick big-time.

The other guys had left earlier that morning to watch NFL games at the other Centerville Prep house. It was just Kelvin and me left, both of us moping at the kitchen table—Kelvin because he had played poorly the night before, me because I was worried I might never get to play again.

"Don't worry about it, man," I said to Kelvin. He had tried to cheer me up earlier in the week, so I thought I should do the same for him. "It's just one game. You'll bounce back."

Kelvin was dejectedly flipping a spoon around in his bowl of half-eaten Cheerios.

He looked like he was going to burst into tears. "You don't get it," he said. "I can't afford any bad games. That's what Coach always says..."

"At least you played," I said. "I've been glued to the bench so far this season. Coach likes you. I can tell."

"I've seen what happens when kids don't play well," Kelvin said sullenly. "They don't last. One day you wake up and they're gone. Coach brings in another kid to take their place."

I gave that comment some deep thought. If anybody was going to be replaced on this team, it would probably be Billy and me. I mean, Coach obviously didn't think we could play.

"You're a star," I said, looking straight at Kelvin. "No way is Coach getting rid of you."

"He ain't getting rid of you," Kelvin shot back. "You're one of the money kids. He might not play you, but he wants your tuition."

"Well, doesn't he want yours?" I said. I wasn't sure what Kelvin was getting at.

"I'm on scholarship," he said. "Thomas, me, Stef and Jabari—we been with Coach for a long time. We don't pay. We play. Coach said we're gonna get scholarships. That's my only chance, man. If I don't get a scholarship, I'll end up back home. There's nothing there for me. I just got to play better."

I could feel the angst in Kelvin's voice. I felt really bad for the kid. There seemed to be so much pressure on him. On the other hand, it was becoming clear to me exactly where I stacked up in this whole Centerville Prep basketball scenario. I—or more accurately, my parents—were footing the bill for some of these other kids who weren't paying at all.

I still believed that I was a good basketball player. But I was beginning to seriously wonder whether Coach Stone had ever really thought so. What Kelvin had just revealed made me very, very suspicious of Coach's motives. Had he come to Midland last year to recruit a basketball player for his prep school or to find a sucker to help cover the bills?

A rough draft of my first creative-writing assignment was due the next day, so I tried to push all those thoughts out of my head. What good would stewing about it do anyway? And besides, I still wanted to play for Centerville. The basketball was great, and no coach was going to tell me I wasn't a legitimate college prospect. Still, even though I tried, I couldn't help but dwell on the whole big mess.

The creative-writing assignment was to write the opening chapter of our own novel. I hadn't even attended a class yet because of my late entry, but Mr. Jenkins had forwarded me the details by email. We were allowed to write about any topic we wanted. *As long as it grabs readers and doesn't let them go*, wrote the teacher. That was a funny way of putting it, I thought.

The only thing that was "grabbing" me at the moment was my stewing over the situation at Centerville, Coach Stone and how upset my parents would be when they found out how this "first-class prep school" wasn't living up to the hype. Then I got an idea—I'd write some "fiction" about precisely that.

Two furious hours of writing later, I had my rough draft completely done. It was even longer than required, coming in at precisely 1,249 words. My fictional character was Gus, a kid who had joined a prep basketball program in Akron, Ohio. Those details were made up. But the story about how the prep school hadn't exactly lived up to its advance billing was all too real. I chuckled to myself as I finished. At least my frustration was paying off by making my homework a little easier.

Chapter Eight

Creative writing was actually turning out to be an interesting class. I liked the way Mr. Jenkins talked to us, taking the poem "Daffodils" by William Wordsworth and dissecting each line. We had all read the short poem at the start of class, and I liked the images it conjured in my head. But Mr. Jenkins was showing us deeper meanings in each line that hadn't dawned on me as I was reading it. He was really passionate about what he was teaching. Just like a good coach.

The class flew by, and before I knew it, the clock on the wall showed three o'clock. I realized that I had been so engrossed in the lecture, I had forgotten about basketball practice and the fact that I would be late getting to it today.

When the final bell sounded, I grabbed my backpack, slung it over one shoulder and headed toward the door. It would be about a twenty-minute walk to the rec center if I hurried. I figured I would miss only about a half hour of practice.

"Hold on a second." Mr. Jenkins was motioning for me to come over to his desk. "We haven't met," said the thin, sandy-haired man with horn-rimmed glasses. "You must be Jake?"

"Yes," I said. "I missed last week's class because—"

"Oh, that's okay. Ms. Munoz told me you were a late registrant. Something about a mix-up with the prep basketball program.

Don't worry about that. We're just getting started here anyway."

"Okay, thanks. I have to head to practice," I said.

"I just wanted to give you some feedback on your rough draft," Mr. Jenkins said. "It's very good, you know. You made it seem so real."

My cheeks flushed. "Thanks," I stammered. If only he knew the half of it.

I hurried out the door and began walking at a brisk pace toward the Benson Recreation Center. I knew I'd better get there as soon as possible. No sense giving Coach anything more to be angry with me about.

At the pace I was walking, it actually only took me fifteen minutes to reach the rec center. As I made my way up the stairs, I noticed a white van parked in front of the building. The side of the van read *State Board of Education*. Two men were sitting in the front seat, talking as they read over some papers. One of them looked familiar to me, but I wasn't sure why.

I rushed up the steps, through the reception area and down to the locker room. I hurriedly pulled on my practice gear and high-tops and headed out onto the court. Coach was running the guys through our 2-2-1 press. Without me, there were still ten guys—enough to put two full teams on the floor—so at least my being late hadn't disrupted practice.

"Well, nice of you to grace us with your presence, Midland," Coach bellowed across the floor. There he went again, using that nickname. I was beginning to really hate it when he did that. "Where have you been, Burnett? How can I be expected to run a practice when players don't even show up on time? And you wonder why you don't play."

"But Coach—" I began.

"No excuses," he growled. "Get on the baseline. Because you're late, everybody on the team is going to do three man-makers."

The guys groaned, and a few of them scowled at me. If looks could kill...

We all did three man-makers. This time nobody puked. When we were done,

Coach pointed at me. "You're not finished, Burnett." At least he was using my real name this time. "Give me five more! The rest of you can shoot free throws."

I slogged my way through five more man-makers. I was in good shape, but the last two hurt. I was gasping for air as I finished, and I felt a stitch in my side. "Maybe you'll think twice about being late next time," Coach said.

"But I was at creative-writing class," I said. "I talked to you about it last week. You said it was okay."

Coach just stared at me. It was like I hadn't even said anything. I knew he remembered, but I didn't for a second think he would admit he'd made a mistake in disciplining me and the team.

The rest of the practice went fine. We worked on our press break and our zone offense and did a lot of three-point shooting. We were playing Carson Prep the next day, and they employed primarily zone defense. Coach wanted us to be ready to bust their zone with our long-range perimeter game and good ball movement.

"Okay, fellas, that's it," Coach Stone said. "Pretty decent practice, after Johnny-come-lately arrived."

A few of the guys chuckled. I shrugged it off. At this point, I was getting used to Coach taking shots at me. I headed into the locker room with the guys. We all showered and changed before heading out together to find Coach for a ride home. Even though I didn't like how things had been going for me at Centerville, this was still a solid group of guys to hang out with.

As we entered the gym, I saw Coach talking to two men in dark suits. They were the same ones who had been sitting in the white van out front before practice. And now I remembered how I recognized the one with the salt-and-pepper hair. He had sat next to me on the plane to Union City.

What they were engaged in across the gym didn't appear to be a friendly conversation. Coach was waving his arms around and pointing his finger in the faces of both men. "We better wait a minute," Thomas said, and we all held back. "That doesn't look good."

Coach Stone was now standing with his arms crossed over his chest, staring at the two men. "I don't care what you all say or where you're from! You're not talking to my guys!" He had raised his voice, and his words were clearly audible across the gym. The men turned and walked out of the building. I got the distinct sense from their body language that they were not satisfied.

Coach strode across the floor toward us. "Let's get going, boys," he said. "I've got stuff to do tonight."

Thomas had a worried expression on his normally relaxed face. "What's up, Coach?" he said. "What did they want?"

"How about you let me worry about that?" Coach shot back. "You all just worry about basketball and getting ready for Carson tomorrow." It was pretty clear from Coach's demeanor that the subject was closed.

I could tell that Coach Stone didn't consider Carson much of a threat to us. Unlike our previous opponents to date, Carson didn't have a single dominating player. From the look of their warm-up at the other end of the floor, they were a bunch of white guys who were all about the same height. Nobody on the team was intimidating in size or in skill. The crowd at our home court was about half the size it had been for Skyline. Meanwhile, our guys, particularly the starters, didn't seem to have a lot of jump during warm-up either.

Our low energy carried over from warm-up into the game. Instead of dominating from the start as our first five had before, they had trouble in the opening minutes simply completing passes against Carson's pesky, disciplined zone defense. The visitors were "firing" on Thomas in the post, meaning they were rushing a second defender in on him whenever he caught the ball inside. Thomas wasn't able to score with the ease he had shown in our previous games. And when he made the right play out of the double team and kicked the ball out to a shooter, our guys weren't hitting. By the end of the first quarter, Kelvin had made just two of six threes, while Joey and Jabari had gone scoreless. For the first time this year, we trailed after a quarter with Carson ahead 22–16.

"What is wrong with you guys!" Coach screamed at the guards in the huddle. "You're getting easy shots and you're not stepping up. Hell, even I could make those shots."

As if to prove his point, Coach looked down the bench. "Billy, Jake—take out Kelvin and Joey," he said, glaring at both of them. "You two have a seat!"

Billy was in shock. I suppose I must have worn the same stunned look on my face. But I whipped off my warm-up top and ran to the scorer's table. I wasn't about to let Coach change his mind. Billy was right behind me.

It was Carson's ball to start the second quarter. I lined up against Steve Sylvester, a guard about my size who was likely their best player. He dribbled upcourt slowly. I got into a stance with my head on the ball as every coach had taught me since night league. Sylvester tried to cross me over, but I anticipated it and stole the ball. Thomas instinctively ran the court and was loping well ahead of his man. I didn't think—I just tossed the ball up toward the hoop. Thomas rose and rose, catching the ball and slamming it through the hoop in one beautiful motion.

"That's it, Burnett!" Coach yelled from the sideline. "That's the way!" It was the first positive comment he'd directed my way since I'd arrived at Centerville.

A few minutes later I found myself open on the wing as the ball moved into Thomas in the post. The defense collapsed on him, and the big fella fired a perfect pass out to me on the perimeter. Again, my instinct took over. I launched the shot. Nothing but net. My first shot for Centerville was a money three.

We had stormed ahead 32-26 by this point. The Carson bench called a timeout to stop the bleeding. I was pumped! I was actually leading a comeback for us. Just contributing and playing felt so good.

It didn't last long. In the timeout, Coach glanced down the bench. "Kelvin, Joey, you're back in for Billy and Jake."

I couldn't help but be disappointed as the game resumed. I had played well—great, even—and now here I was, back on the bench. Billy had touched the ball only once, bobbling it off his shoe and out of bounds. But I felt I'd made the most of my chance. Surely I would get back on, wouldn't I?

As it turned out, the answer was no. Not for this game. Reinvigorated and maybe feeling a little threatened as they returned to the lineup, Kelvin and Joey caught fire. They began hitting threes and feeding Thomas and Stef on backdoor cuts. The rout was on. We wound up winning going away, taking the game by a 65–38 margin. But Billy and I never saw the floor again.

When I checked my email before bed, a message was waiting for me. I didn't immediately recognize the name. It was from bjennings@sboe.com. The subject line read *Urgent, Please Read!* I was tempted to delete it, thinking it was a scam or a virus. But for some reason I changed my mind and opened it.

Jake,

My name is Bill Jennings. We met on the airplane to Union City last week, and I enjoyed talking with you. I am writing you now about something serious though.

As I mentioned on the plane, I work for the State Board of Education. One of the things I do is check out schools to make sure they are fully compliant with our standards and curriculum. I had never heard of Centerville Prep until I met you, which is strange when you consider what I do for a living. So I started looking into the program, and I developed some serious concerns about Centerville, on a number of levels. My understanding from speaking with your counselor at Roosevelt, Ms. Munoz, is that you might have some of the same concerns.

Would you be willing to speak with me about this in person? I can assure you that the process would be strictly confidential. I can understand how you might be worried about that.

We believe that what Irvine Stone is doing with Centerville Prep is not entirely above-board, and it is critical that we speak with some of his players. As one of those players, we believe it is important that you look out for your best interests.

Please contact me at this email address.

Sincerely,
Bill Jennings
Superintendent of Academic Regulation
State Board of Education

I gulped, needing to read the email twice to make sure I wasn't seeing things. So this was what the visit to our practice had been about. It seemed like I wasn't the only one who thought Centerville Prep wasn't living up to its advertising. But what was I going to do about this? I didn't like the idea of ratting out Coach, even if he had treated me badly. And what would happen to my teammates if the state shut down Centerville? What would happen to kids like Kelvin and Thomas?

I closed the email and shut down my computer. I had no clue what to do about it. I only knew I wanted to make sure nobody else in the house saw the email. Normally, I would have talked with my parents about something like this. But they weren't here. And besides, how could I talk to them about the problems at Centerville after I'd been telling them since I arrived how great things were?

I decided to sleep on it. But it took at least an hour of tossing and turning before I drifted off. So many scenarios were running through my mind—none of them ending in a positive way.

Chapter Nine

I was already awake when the alarm clock went off at seven on Friday morning. Thomas was still sleeping, and so were the other guys in the house, so I decided to beat the rush for the shower. I hadn't been able to sleep much the past couple of nights as I wrestled with what to do. It was while I was lathering up with shampoo that I made my decision. I would talk to Coach Stone about the email from the State Board of Education.

It was only fair. I was part of the team. Even though things hadn't quite gone as planned, I couldn't just turn on Coach and my teammates. That wasn't what I had learned through a dozen years of playing all kinds of organized sports. Coach Irvine Stone, as the email had referred to him, deserved a chance to explain himself.

I didn't have a class in last period on Friday, so I made sure to get to the parking lot that afternoon before all the other guys. Maybe if Coach showed up with the van early, we could talk. Just as I'd hoped, he rolled in at about ten after two, a few minutes before the rest of the team would arrive.

"You're early today," Coach said.

"Yeah, I wanted to talk to you," I replied. Might as well get straight to it.

"What about?"

"I got an email this week," I said. I was nervous. It wasn't easy bringing up something this sensitive with Coach. "It was from the State Board of Education. They want to talk with me about Centerville Prep."

Coach drew a heavy sigh and ran a hand through what was left of his hair. I could tell my comment had made him uncomfortable. A bead of sweat trickled down his face, past his left ear.

"What did it say exactly?"

I had actually printed out a copy, so I handed it to him. Coach's brow furrowed as he read the email. He was shaking his head as he got to the end.

"You know this is a load of crap," he said, looking carefully at me.

"Yeah, but..."

"But what?"

"Well, this program—Centerville Prep—isn't exactly the way you described it to me and my parents," I said. Oh boy, I had opened it up now. "I mean, I wasn't even registered for the courses you told me I could take. We don't live in dorms. There's never enough food. We're going to a public school..."

Just then Thomas and Kelvin rounded the corner from the school into the parking lot.

"Look, let's talk about this later, okay?" Coach said, eyeing the other guys. He was almost pleading.

"All right," I said. Only I didn't feel all right about it. Not at all.

I thought about nothing else all practice. I couldn't concentrate. Shots I would normally knock down were hitting front rim or were total air balls. I was bobbling passes, and Kelvin was beating me to the rim badly. Luckily, Coach didn't seem to notice. No man-makers for me or the team today.

We didn't have a game till the following Tuesday, so as practice winded down, Coach gathered us together. "Take the weekend off," he said. "We've had a lot of basketball in a very short period of time. Relax, do some homework, go to a movie or something. Recharge."

The guys were clearly happy about this as we headed home in the van. Even though we all loved basketball, an entire weekend without practice sounded pretty appealing right now. Coach dropped the guys from the other house off first, which differed from his usual routine. He then backtracked and took us to our place. He stopped in front of the house, and we were all piling out when Coach Stone spoke. "Jake, hold up a minute."

The other guys were already heading up the sidewalk. I stayed in the backseat of the van with the sliding door half open. Coach shut off the ignition and turned to face me.

"Jake, I'm not perfect, I'll admit that," he began. I wondered what was coming next.

"But I think we've got a good thing going here. We've definitely got a great team. I'm trying to do my best for all you boys. I know some things about Centerville are not what you thought they were going to be. But you have to believe me when I say I wasn't trying to mislead you or your parents. I thought we would be in a dorm, and I thought I had a deal with Benson Catholic for you guys to attend private school. But it fell through at the last minute.

"The point is, the basketball is good, right?"

I nodded. The basketball was good, for sure.

"And I think it will be better for you, now that you're used to my system," Coach continued. "I think you'll see that before long you're going to be getting some interest from college coaches too."

This part took me by complete surprise. College interest! That was great. That was why I was here, after all.

"You really think so, Coach?" I said. "I mean, that would be awesome."

Coach Stone smiled. "Definitely," he said. "But in order for that to happen, we have to stick together. I'm not asking you to do anything wrong. But if you could just hold off talking to that guy who sent you the email, just for a while, it would give me a chance to make sure all the loose ends around Centerville Prep are taken care of. I mean, we don't want to do anything that will get in the way of a national prep title or scholarships for all you guys, do we?"

"No," I said. I meant it. I didn't want to screw things up for anybody, including me.

"Good then, we have an agreement," Coach said. I nodded.

I got out of the van feeling a lot better than I had the day before. At least I had addressed the issue with Coach. What he had said seemed reasonable. And I was happy to hear he still thought college teams would be interested in me.

"Jake," Coach called out as I headed up the sidewalk to the house. He was motioning for me to come over to the driver's side window. He had a hundred-dollar bill in his hand. "Make sure all the guys get to a movie this weekend, on me."

On Saturday all the guys from both houses went to see the latest Wayans brothers flick. It was laughably bad, but we had a blast anyway, joking all the way to and from the theater. The only kid who wasn't having a great time was Billy. He was clearly miserable, walking about twenty feet behind the rest of us. He had his head down as he trudged along, and didn't speak at all.

I dropped back to walk with him. "What's up?" I asked. "You okay?"

Billy shook his head. "The counselor told me yesterday that I'm three credits short of being able to graduate this year," he said. "My mom and dad are going to kill me. I talked them into sending me to this place, and now I'm not even going to graduate. My dad will be so pissed."

"Can't you pick up those courses?" I said. "Ms. Munoz helped me straighten it out. Otherwise, it would have been the same for me."

Again Billy shook his head. "I need college-entrance math, and it's too late to get into it now. She said I'm too far behind. I'll need to take it in summer school, and that won't work to get me into the college my dad wants me in by next fall. I haven't told my parents yet. I'm screwed."

I didn't know what to say. Even though he was from the other house, I felt a certain bond with Billy. Neither of us had played much for Coach Stone. In fact, we seemed to be the only guys on the outside of his rotation looking in. "Just hang in there," I said. "I'm sure your parents will understand." Only I wasn't so sure.

"You don't know my dad," Billy said. "He will absolutely flip out. I talked him into sending me here. He didn't think it was a good idea. He was right. They're coming here next weekend for our two games. He's going to see that I don't even get off the bench. Eventually, he's going to find out that I'm not graduating either. I don't know what to do."

I felt horrible for Billy. He was quiet and awkward and not a great basketball player. But he always worked hard and he seemed like a nice kid. I walked with him in silence until he and the other guys from his house headed out on their own.

Chapter Ten

By the time Monday afternoon's practice rolled around, I was ready for basketball. We'd had the whole weekend off—no shooting, no running through plays, no real exercise of any kind. I was full of energy and ready to compete.

Coach Stone brought us together at center court to go over the practice plan. "We're going to switch things up a bit today to make the teams a little more even," he announced. "Jake, you and Kelvin trade places. Jake, you go Red today, and Kelvin, you go White."

I hadn't been expecting this. But I certainly wasn't arguing. Being on the Red team meant I got to at least practice with Thomas and Stef and the rest of the first-stringers. I was happy, but I could tell by the scowl on his face that Kelvin was just the opposite.

Practicing on the first unit, it was almost like a different game compared to being part of the second-string crew. When we had to break the White team's zone press, it was easy with the huge presence and athleticism of Thomas to pass the ball to in the middle. When we ran our offense against the Whites, it was a pleasure executing pick-and-rolls with Thomas and Stef and finding Joey and Jabari for open looks from three.

We ended the practice with a ten-minute running-time scrimmage. I nailed a three myself, hit Joey for two wide-open jumpers and fed Thomas for a dunk on a beautiful backdoor cut. We killed White, winning

22-6. Only Kelvin's two threes got them on the scoreboard at all.

"Looking good, Red," Coach yelled as practice wrapped up. "Looking very good."

We gathered again at center court. Coach said a few words about Miller Prep, where we would be playing the next day. It was about a thirty-minute drive northeast of Benson. Coach would be picking us up from our houses between 4:00 and 4:30 PM.

"Anyone know where Billy is today?" Coach asked just before we broke for the locker room. I hadn't even noticed that Billy wasn't at practice.

"He said he was sick this morning," Stef said. "Didn't come to school with us."

Back at the house that night, I joined in with the other guys playing *2K*. I was in a great mood. Practice had gone well— easily the best session for me since I had arrived at Centerville. Coach hadn't called me Midland a single time. In fact, he had even complimented me on a couple of my passes and my defense.

By 10:00 PM I was still glowing but exhausted from the two-and-a-half-hour practice. I needed a glass of water before bed. When I entered the kitchen, I found Kelvin sitting alone at the table, looking dejected.

"You all right?" I asked.

"Nah, man. Today sucked," Kelvin said. "I've never been put on the second string by Coach before."

This was awkward. My practice with the first unit had come at the expense of Kelvin, who was likely my best friend on the team. I hadn't thought much about how that affected him until now.

"I'm sure it was just temporary," I said, although inside I hoped that wasn't true— which made me feel guilty about being two-faced.

"We'll see," Kelvin said as he headed off to bed. "We'll see."

I turned on my laptop before climbing into bed. When I checked my email, I saw another message from bjennings@sboe.com. This time the subject line read *My Previous Request*. The email was shorter.

Jake,

I hope you're giving my previous request some serious consideration.

I know you're in a difficult situation. But speaking with us could make a big difference to your future and to your teammates' futures.

Please email me anytime.

Bill Jennings

I felt a pang of guilt that I hadn't responded to the first email. Even just to say no thanks. Obviously, Mr. Jennings wasn't letting this issue go. But what could I do about it? I was just a kid, and Coach had said he only needed a little bit of time to tie up some details at Centerville. I wondered now what those details were. But surely a couple more days wouldn't matter.

We were on the court, warming up for the Miller Prep game, while Coach sat on our bench, filling out the lineup. "Anybody know where Billy is today?" he yelled.

"Still sick," Stef replied. "Didn't go to school today either. Didn't even get out of bed this morning."

Coach raised his eyebrows. "Okay, well, I guess we'll just have to manage without him." His voice had a ring of sarcasm. He'd only played Billy for a few minutes in one game. He was probably glad the kid wasn't here, I thought. It was just one less thing for him to have to think about.

Miller was somewhere between Skyline and Carson in terms of overall talent and size. If we played well, we shouldn't have a problem with them. It was thirty seconds till tip, and Coach wanted us organized on the bench. "Thomas, Stef, Jabari, Joey and Jake—you guys are starting."

Wait—had he actually said my name? I was starting? I knew I'd had a good prac-tice the night before, but I hadn't expected this. Immediately, I sat on one of the five chairs in front of coach—right between Thomas and Stef. A forlorn-looking Kelvin took my usual spot, standing behind Coach. He didn't look me in the eye.

"Okay, you guys. Play hard, play like you're capable of, and we should have no problem. We're in man defense to start—just match up when you get out there. On offense, let's begin with fist, okay?"

Fist was our high pick-and-roll offensive series. Since I was the starting point guard, I would be running it with Thomas and Stef. I was pumped beyond belief for this opportunity.

Thomas won the tip, flicking it back to Joey, who passed it to me. I dribbled across the midcourt line. This was just how I had pictured things before coming to Centerville. Me at the controls of this powerful offense. I noticed that Thomas's man was overplaying him. Immediately I called, "Fist out," which meant that the three other guys were to spot up on the perimeter. Thomas knew what I was thinking. He flashed up hard, like I was going to pass to him in the high post. His defender bit on the fake, lunging for the ball.

Only I wasn't throwing it. Thomas reversed his tracks and headed to the basket. I lobbed it up for him, and the big kid snagged the ball with his massive right hand before crashing down a tomahawk dunk for our first two points. What a start!

That one play seemed to both set the tone for the game and deflate Miller Prep. Through the first quarter, they barely put up any resistance. After ten minutes we led 26–6. Thomas had ten easy points and I had six on a pair of three-pointers after terrific kickouts from the post. I also had three assists. This was more like it.

Coach subbed me out for Kelvin in the second quarter, and the Centerville onslaught continued. Kelvin broke free on the fast break for his own sizzling dunk, which even got some "oohs" and "aahs" from the home Miller crowd. It was pretty impressive to see a five-foot-eight kid throw down like that. I felt good for Kelvin, who had been having a tough week till now. I played the entire third quarter, scoring six more points on another three and an and-one layup, and dishing out five more assists. Kelvin played the fourth quarter.

As the final buzzer sounded, we had won easily with an 88–58 score. I finished with twelve points and eight assists while committing only one turnover. For the first time since arriving at Centerville Prep, I felt really good about my game. Like college coaches might actually be interested in me after all.

Coach Stone was all smiles in the locker room afterward. "Great performance, fellas," he said. "Looks like we got a nice point-guard platoon going in Kelvin and Jake!"

Coach then turned to me. "Didn't I tell you everything would work out?" he said, looking hard at me. "We just got to stick together, right?"

I nodded. He was staring at me so intensely, it was uncomfortable. I didn't really understand why.

It all became clear as we left the locker room to go back to the van. That's when I noticed the two men from the State Board of Education. They had come all the way to Miller to watch our game. Had they come here to talk to me?

Coach grabbed my arm as we walked out of the gym together. Bill Jennings caught my eye as we strode past him. He mouthed the words *We need to talk*. Coach tightened his grip and ushered me out to the van.

I wondered why these guys were so persistent in trying to talk to me. Hadn't they taken the hint? I didn't want to talk to them. Not if it meant it would hurt the Centerville program and my teammates. Especially not now that I was finally getting a chance to prove I was a legitimate player.

The guys were in a great mood again as we headed home toward Benson on the freeway. I felt my iPhone buzzing in my pocket. I figured it was probably Mom and Dad. I had promised to call them after the game. But there hadn't been time before we left the gym, especially not with Coach hurrying us out like that.

It wasn't a call though. It was a text. From Billy. And all it said was, **Thanks for**

being my friend. Nothing else. This was weird. Billy had never texted me before. He'd only called me once. Why was he thanking me for being his friend? It didn't make much sense.

The other guys' house was closer to the Benson freeway exit, so Coach turned down their street to drop them off first. As we approached their house, we saw the flashing red lights of an ambulance and a police car parked outside. What was going on? Was there a fire?

Just as we pulled up behind the police car, paramedics emerged from the front door with a stretcher. Somebody was lying on it, an IV sticking out of his arm. "It's Billy," shouted Jabari. "What the hell is going on?"

Coach jumped out of the van. The rest of us followed. A police officer tried to stop Coach from getting too close. "It's okay. I am this boy's coach. I rent the house he lives in," Coach said.

The officer pulled Coach Stone aside and turned to us. "Boys, can you please get back in the van?" We turned around and piled into the vehicle.

After a few minutes the ambulance pulled away from the house, Billy in the back. Coach and the police officer were talking. Coach walked slowly back to the van with a piece of paper in his hand.

"What happened?" Jabari asked.

"I got a damn ticket," Coach said. "Too many of us in this vehicle for the number of seat belts. We'll be okay on the ride home, though, once you boys from this house get out."

"But what happened to Billy?" Jabari pressed. "Where are they taking him?"

"Billy is sick," Coach said. "He's really not feeling well. But don't worry—it's not serious, and it's not contagious. They're taking him to hospital as a precaution."

The guys from the other house jumped out of the vehicle. It was a relief to all of us that Billy was okay. Coach drove the rest of us to our house and dropped us off.

"Jake," he said to me. "Good job tonight."

"Thanks."

"And good job getting out of the gym without talking to those guys. I appreciate it."

Coach drove away. With Billy going off in the ambulance, I had forgotten all about the State Board of Education. But something about the way Coach had handled things tonight was gnawing at me. He hadn't seemed too concerned with how Billy was doing. In fact, he seemed more worried about the ticket the cops had handed him. But he was obviously most concerned about the possibility of me talking to Bill Jennings.

Chapter Eleven

It was already 9:30 PM and I should have been tired, but so much had happened that night. I wasn't anywhere close to being ready for bed. I was still excited about the game but troubled about Coach and Centerville. And despite what Coach had said about Billy, I was especially worried about him.

Kelvin and I were sitting at the kitchen table when I got an idea. "Hey, do you want to go see if we can visit Billy?"

"You mean in the hospital?"

"Yeah. I mean, the kid is all alone here. He'd probably really appreciate it."

Kelvin grabbed his jacket, and so did I. I had noticed Benson General on our daily drives with Coach to the rec center. It was going to be quite a hike, and I wasn't sure when the buses were running.

"Let's take a cab," I said. "I still have some emergency money from my parents."

We called a taxi, and just a half hour later we pulled up to the front doors of the hospital. I wasn't sure where Billy would be. I went to the main reception desk, with Kelvin right behind me.

"Can I help you?" asked the woman with a phone headset who was sitting at the desk.

"We're trying to find our friend—our teammate," I said. "He's sick, and they brought him here by ambulance tonight."

"What's his name?" she asked. "We get quite a few ambulances in here."

"It's Billy." Suddenly I realized I didn't even know his last name. "I'm sorry—that's all I know."

The attendant looked confused. "Well, we had a boy about your age brought in here an hour or so ago, but he's in the ICU," she said. "And you can't visit patients in ICU."

I knew what ICU stood for—intensive care unit. If that boy was Billy, this wasn't good news. "How do we get there?"

"Fourth floor," she said. "But like I said, you won't be able to visit..."

Kelvin and I were already on our way to the elevators. Once we reached the fourth floor, I looked for another reception desk. I found one, but there was nobody staffing it.

We walked down a hallway, peering into each room as we passed it. In the third one, I spotted the floppy red hair of Billy. He was asleep, an IV tube still sticking out of his right arm. He looked even more pale than usual.

"You guys shouldn't be in here!" The stern voice of the ICU nurse startled me.

"Sorry," I said. "This is our teammate."

"Oh," the nurse said. "We've been looking for somebody who knows this boy.

The paramedics got ID from his wallet, and we've finally managed to locate his parents by phone. But they're from out of state and won't be able to get here until tomorrow."

"What's wrong with him?" I asked.

"Well, that's what we're trying to find out," she said. "He was apparently alone in the house, so the paramedics couldn't get any more information. But we do know he's been drinking. And it seems he's taken a lot of pills."

What? Was she serious? Billy seemed like such a straitlaced kid. And what did she mean by *a lot of pills*? What was going on here?

"What kind of pills?" I asked. "Is he going to be all right?"

"It was touch and go for a bit," she said gently. "I'm not sure exactly what he took. But we pumped his stomach, and I think he'll make a full recovery. He's lucky. He may not be in too good of shape for the next few days though."

The nurse asked us who Billy's guardian in Benson was, and why he was at the house by himself. We told her about Centerville Prep and explained that Coach Stone was responsible for all of us. But where was he? Hadn't he even bothered to check up on one of his players who was taken to hospital in an ambulance?

Kelvin gave her Coach's cell number. The nurse then turned to us.

"Billy is lucky he has good friends like you two," she said. "But it's time for you both to go home. He won't be doing any talking with anybody tonight. Maybe you can come back tomorrow."

Kelvin and I were pretty quiet in the cab on the way back to the house. But just before we got to the front door, he turned to me. "Coach is in major trouble, isn't he?"

I hadn't been thinking about Coach, with Billy in the hospital, but I knew Kelvin was right. And now I was seriously wondering if agreeing not to talk to the State Board of Education had been the right thing to do.

Sleep was a long time coming that night, even though I was exhausted from the day's events. The game against Miller seemed long ago now. In fact, basketball didn't even seem important. All I could think about was Billy. Kelvin and I hadn't talked about it, but I knew what the ICU nurse was saying. Alcohol and pills. What happened to Billy hadn't been an accident. He had been trying to kill himself.

Chapter Twelve

I had one class the next morning, but I decided to skip it. I told Kelvin and Thomas that I had a spare and was going to do some schoolwork at home. But once they left for Roosevelt, I grabbed my coat. I was going back to the hospital.

This time, I walked. It only took forty-five minutes to get there. I checked with the receptionist and found out Billy had been moved to a general ward on the third floor. I headed to his room immediately.

Morning visiting hours went until 10:30. I had fifteen minutes to check in on him.

Billy was awake when I entered the room. His mop of red hair rested on the white pillow. He was still very pale, which made his freckles pop out even more than usual. I thought his blue eyes brightened a bit when he saw me enter the room. But overall, the kid looked really down.

"Hey," I said gently. This was awkward.

"Hey," he replied wearily. Billy seemed nervous too.

"What happened, man?" I asked.

Billy's eyes began to water, and then he started to sob quietly. I put a hand on his arm.

"I...I just didn't know what else to do," he said. "There was no way out. There still isn't..."

"Dude, it's never that bad," I said.

"It's bad. My parents are on their way here from Galveston. Now my dad will think I'm a total loser. And he still doesn't even know about the school thing."

"Look," I said. "I know you're feeling low. But promise me you won't do anything like this again. We could have talked. You could have called me. The point is, you're not alone. And I'm sure your parents will understand."

"Thanks," Billy said. "But basketball has been my whole life, man. I thought going to Centerville Prep would pretty much guarantee me a scholarship. Now I don't even get off the bench, I'm not going to graduate, and my dad is going to be pissed after paying $35,000 for me to come here."

"It's going to be okay," I said. "Look, basketball isn't everything. You've got a lot of things going for you. The most important thing now is that you get healthy and that you stay positive."

Billy managed a weak smile. I thought maybe I had made him feel a little better—at least, not so all alone anyway. An announcement came over the hospital PA system that visiting hours were over.

"I've got to go," I said. "But I'll be back. So take it easy, and remember what I said."

As I left the hospital, my mind was racing. Mostly, I was pissed at Coach for lying about Centerville Prep, taking advantage of Billy and getting him into this bind. But I was also confused. I had just told Billy that basketball wasn't everything, and I had actually meant it. There were more important things in life—like being happy, being a good friend, living up to your word and doing the right thing. As I neared the school, I realized I had made my decision.

Before going to business class, I ducked into the library and pulled out my laptop. I composed a new email. It was brief and to the point.

Mr. Jennings,

I'm sorry I haven't got back to you about this. I had to think it over. But now I've decided that I will speak to you.

When and where can we meet?

Thanks,
Jake

I was preoccupied with thoughts about Billy and the State Board of Education as

I entered Ms. Cuthbert's business class. But the subject matter in her class for the day was appropriate. She was teaching us more about contracts and the remedies when somebody breaks a deal. One of those remedies was legal action.

"If somebody can prove that they were harmed by the other party not fulfilling a contract, that is grounds for legal action," Ms. Cuthbert told the class.

That got me thinking. Coach Stone certainly hadn't lived up to his end of the bargain. Maybe my parents, and especially Billy's parents, could sue to recover our money. And speaking of money, what had Billy meant about his Dad shelling out $35,000? My parents had paid $22,000 for the school year. I knew Kelvin's family hadn't paid anything, and I doubted Thomas's had either. I was beginning to realize that Coach was making this all up on the fly.

Maybe I hadn't wanted to consider it before, but it was also dawning on me that my sudden increase in playing time and my starting role in the previous game were just a little too coincidental. I still believed I was a good basketball player. But why had Coach changed his mind about me so quickly? If I was being really honest with myself, there was only one good reason. He was trying to buy my silence.

I checked my email again following the business class. There was already a reply from Bill Jennings.

Jake,

Are you able to meet me today at 1 pm? I can come to the school. Please text and let me know.

Bill

He left his cell number at the bottom of the email. I would meet him. I knew now it was the right thing to do.

Mr. Jennings had the same friendly smile on his face that I remembered from the flight to Union City. That put me at ease as we met in the courtyard at Roosevelt.

"Thanks for agreeing to see me, Jake," he said. "I'll get right to the point. The State Board of Education has been investigating Centerville Prep. We've had complaints from teachers here at Roosevelt about academic irregularities on many of the players' transcripts and about their enrollment here at Roosevelt. Frankly, the academic side of Centerville Prep is a complete shambles. We've examined in detail each of the player's school records, and you are the only one who is even on track to graduate this year."

I gulped. I was only "on track" because I had been lucky enough to make an appointment with Ms. Munoz shortly after arriving. The situation was worse than I thought.

"But why did you want to talk to me?" I said. "Why not any of the other players?"

"Ms. Munoz and Mr. Jenkins contacted us," he explained. "Mr. Jenkins told us about your paper. About the 'fictional' basketball prep school you wrote about. Many of the details sounded similar to the way we understand Coach Stone has operated over the past few years. We felt you would be a good person to talk to, seeing as you're new and not one of the kids Coach Stone has had with him for a while.

"We need a student to testify to really make our investigation stick. We know things aren't right at Centerville, that Coach Stone has put a lot of kids in academic jeopardy. Honestly, he's put kids' safety at risk, too, leaving you all unsupervised in those houses and without enough food. What happened to Billy could have ended up much, much worse."

I knew Mr. Jennings was right. Billy had been lucky.

"The State Department of Child and Family Services is also involved now," Mr. Jennings continued. "So are the police, because Coach Stone has failed to pay many of his bills, including a sizable tab at the Metro Diner."

Mr. Jennings looked at me intently.

"I don't know," I said. "It would kind of be like ratting out Coach and the rest of the guys."

"That's one way to look at it," he said. "The other way to look at it is that Coach Stone has basically been stealing from families like yours and Billy's. He's been selling a dream that too many people have bought into. All he wants is for one of these kids, like Thomas Delane, to make it to the NBA, and then he'll leech off that kid for the rest of his life. To call Centerville a prep school is a farce. And Coach Stone is a fraud."

My head was reeling. This was a lot to think about.

"Can I let you know tomorrow?" I asked.

"Sure," Mr. Jennings said. "Text me. That's the quickest."

Practice that afternoon was really difficult for me. I had trouble concentrating. I couldn't look Coach Stone and the rest of the players in the eye. I felt like a traitor. Had I really done the right thing by talking to Mr. Jennings?

I was just settling into my math homework that evening when my cell rang.

"Hi, Jake." It was Dad. This was weird. Mom was the one who always called, followed by Dad picking up the extension in the bedroom. This time it was the opposite.

"Are you okay?" he continued. "We got a call from your school counselor. She told us about what's going on at Centerville."

I was panicking now. How much did Mom and Dad know?

"Ms. Munoz emailed us a copy of your paper," Dad said. "She thinks it's more than fiction. Jake, you have to be honest with us. What's going on there?"

There was no sense holding anything back. Over the next few minutes, I poured it out to Mom and Dad. I told them everything. I told them how we were all actually attending a public school. How I hadn't been enrolled in journalism or fine arts. How I was living in a house with five other players and how the food was scarce. I told them about Billy and about talking to the State Board of Education.

"I'm really sorry," I said. "I just didn't know how to tell you guys. I wanted

Centerville to be great. I know you spent a ton of money on sending me here. I just didn't know what to say..."

Dad cleared his throat. "It's okay, Jake," he said. "I wish you would have come to us about this, but I understand it must have been difficult. I know how much you love basketball."

I was relieved. I was so happy that my dad was more understanding than Billy's.

"Jake, we think you should come home," Mom said. "Dad will talk to a lawyer about what we can do about the money, but I suspect Coach Stone has a few people looking for cash from him. What's really important is to get you back to Midland as soon as possible."

A few weeks earlier, those would have been the last words I wanted to hear. But now, after everything that had happened, I couldn't disagree. I realized now how much I missed home.

"We'll get you a plane ticket for tomorrow night," Dad said. "I'll text you the details."

After I said goodbye to my parents, I realized I had to act quickly. I texted Mr. Jennings. **I've decided to testify. Can we meet tomorrow?**

His reply came seconds later. **Excellent. Thanks. I'll meet you at school at 1 pm.**

Talking to Mom and Dad had put things into perspective for me even more. I had no choice but to speak to the State Board of Education. For Billy's sake, and for the sake of all the other players and families who were being used by Coach Stone. Despite all that was going on, that night I slept better than I had in a week.

Chapter Thirteen

Mr. Jennings met me in the counselor's office at Roosevelt the next afternoon. His partner was with him, carrying a small digital recorder.

"Jake, this is Frank Bracco," he said. "He will be recording our conversation, as it is on the record and may be used in a case against Coach Stone."

"Okay," I said. I was nervous.

Over the next thirty minutes, Mr. Jennings asked me what I had been promised by

Coach Stone at Centerville and what he had actually delivered. He asked me about my courses and how I had been short the credits needed to graduate before meeting with Ms. Munoz. He asked me about our living conditions at the house. The lack of supervision. The scarcity of food and the transportation to and from practice. Finally, he asked me what I knew about Billy and the night he had been taken to hospital.

"That's it," Mr. Jennings said after the final question had been answered.

Mr. Bracco clicked off the recorder. "Jake, your testimony has really helped. I am confident that we'll be able to shut down Centerville Prep and make sure that Irvine Stone can't pull any more scams like this. At least, not in this state."

I nodded. It was weird. Hearing that Centerville was going to be shut down left me with mixed feelings. I knew it had to be done. But I was sad that our team wouldn't be playing together anymore. And what about the rest of the guys? What about Thomas and Kelvin? What would happen to them?

"Don't worry about your teammates," Mr. Jennings said, sensing my concern. "We'll be in touch with their families. They'll have to sort out their school situations, but they will be free to transfer and play basketball at the high-school level this season in their own communities."

I was relieved to hear that. The last thing I wanted was to mess things up for Thomas and Kelvin and the rest of them by testifying.

"Jake, you did the right thing here," Mr. Jennings said.

I wasn't certain when the other guys on the team would be hearing the news. But I was leaving for Midland that evening on a 9:00 PM flight out of Union City. I wasn't going to simply take off without facing up to them and saying goodbye. It was nearly two o'clock. So I decided to meet them in the parking lot before they left with Coach Stone for practice.

When I got to the parking lot, however, none of the guys were there. This was weird.

Had practice been canceled? I hadn't heard anything about that. I was walking back toward the school to say thanks and goodbye to Ms. Munoz when I saw Thomas and Kelvin approaching me.

"Coach won't be coming today," Thomas said matter-of-factly. "I got a text from him this morning. He left town. Said he's dissolving Centerville. Said he's planning to start another prep school next term. Said he'd be in touch."

I was surprised. Coach Stone must have known that the investigators were closing in on him. Still, that had been an awfully quick getaway. And had he just left all the players—including the kids who had been with him for years—high and dry?

"Guys, I probably should let you know," I said. "Coach left town because he was going to get shut down by the State—"

"We know," Thomas said. "It's not the first time we've been through this kind of thing with Coach. But it will be the last. Kelvin and I are heading home to Missouri.

We've had enough, and so have our parents. There are always lots of promises from that guy, but things never really work out the way he says they will."

I felt bad for those two kids. I was going to miss them, too. They weren't just my teammates—they were good friends.

"It's all good though," Kelvin continued. "Thomas got more than twenty recruiting letters in the last two weeks alone—some from big schools too. Kentucky, Duke, Michigan State...Our boy's going Division 1 once he does some summer school to make up the credits he's missing."

That was awesome. I was confident that someday I'd be watching Thomas Delane play in the NBA too. He was that good.

"Tell him your news, little dude," Thomas said and grinned.

"I definitely got some academics to catch up on too," Kelvin said. "But Turner Junior College wants me for next season. I'm gonna get that scholarship!"

This was terrific news. Of all the kids at Centerville Prep, these two were the ones

I felt closest to. It was a big relief to hear they weren't going to get dragged down by Coach Stone. We shook hands and exchanged hugs in the schoolyard as we said our goodbyes. I sure hoped I would get to see these guys, and maybe even play basketball with them, again.

It didn't take me long to walk to the hospital, even though I was hauling both my backpack and my suitcase with the family tartan luggage tag attached.

When I entered his hospital room, Billy's mom and dad were sitting in chairs beside his bed. His dad was tall, like Billy, with a shock of bright-red hair. He smiled and stuck out his right hand as I entered. "You must be Jake," he said. "I'm Mike Millard, Billy's dad. And this is his mom, Sheila."

I could tell that Billy's mom, a short woman with brown hair and a round face, had been crying. But she smiled warmly and wrapped me in a gentle hug. "Thanks for being here to support our son," she whispered in my ear.

"We're just going to go get a coffee," Billy's dad said. "See you guys in a few minutes."

Billy smiled at me as they left the room. He looked a whole lot better than he had just this morning. I was relieved.

"How's it going?" I asked.

"Way better," he said. "My parents have actually been great. They're not mad at all about the school thing—at least, not mad at me. I feel so stupid that I panicked and did that. It was such a stupid thing. I guess I just didn't see any way out at the time."

"Don't be too tough on yourself," I said. "Coach is the one who put you in that situation. Now he's in big trouble."

"I know. The investigators from the State Board of Education were in here today to talk to us," Billy said. "I'm going back home to Texas tomorrow. I'm really looking forward to that. My parents are going to get me some counseling, maybe find out why all this happened with me.

It's not just about basketball or school. I've been feeling down and really confused off and on for a while now. I think it's a good idea for me to get some help."

"I think so too," I said. "You going to play ball this year at your old school?"

"Maybe. We'll see," Billy said. "You know, I've always played mainly because I was so tall. And because my dad played for the school too. Now I guess I'll just take some time to figure out if it's something I want to keep doing."

I smiled. That made sense. Billy seemed relieved and happier than I had seen him in all our time together at Centerville.

"I'm going home too," I said. "I'm flying out tonight. But you've got my cell. Just text or call if you ever need to talk."

"I will, bro, for sure," Billy said. "And thanks for everything, Jake."

There were several cabs waiting in the hospital parking lot. I hopped into the backseat of one and asked the driver to take me to Benson Station. I glanced at my bright-yellow Midland Tigers backpack resting beside me. Just a few weeks earlier, I couldn't wait to get rid of that thing. Now I couldn't wait to be a Tiger again. Sometimes I guess you don't know how good things are until you don't have them anymore.

I missed Mom and Dad more than I'd ever thought I would. I also missed my friends at Midland. Especially the guys on the basketball team. It would be great to rejoin the squad and graduate from high school with all the people I had grown up with. Until this moment, I hadn't really thought about how weird it would have been not to do that.

I had thought that Centerville Prep was the key to fulfilling all my dreams, to making me a success. But now I realized that I had the strength to do that on my own in Midland. And if basketball didn't work out, I would find something else that made me happy. Just like Billy was going to do. Basketball was a great game, but it didn't define us.

"Where you going, kid?" the cabbie asked, making conversation as he drove to the bus station.

"Home," I said.

That one simple word had never sounded so good.

Acknowledgments

Thanks to Orca Book Publishers, editor Amy Collins and my family for their guidance, expertise, advice and support as I wrote this book.

Jeff Rud was a print journalist in western Canada for twenty-eight years, twenty as a sports writer. He is currently executive director of strategy and communications in British Columbia's Office of the Representative for Children and Youth. This is Jeff's eleventh book and his third novel in the Orca Sports series. He lives in Victoria, British Columbia, with his wife, Lana, and likes to coach high-school basketball in his spare time.

Titles in the Series

orca sports